Come in～♪
La Esperança
エスペランサ
3
かわい千草
Chigusa Kawai

La Esperança

3

Translation	Sachiko Sato
Lettering	Studio Cutie
Graphic Design	Fred Lui / Eric Rosenberger
Editing	Stephanie Donnelly
Editor in Chief	Fred Lui
Publisher	Hikaru Sasahara

English Edition Published by
DIGITAL MANGA PUBLISHING
A division of DIGITAL MANGA, Inc.
1487 W 178th Street, Suite 300
Gardena, CA 90248

www.dmpbooks.com

First Edition: April 2006
ISBN: 1-56970-931-9

1 3 5 7 9 10 8 6 4 2

Printed in China

THIS WAS THE BEGINNING.

予鐘
THE SUMMONING BELL

ARE YOU OKAY?
FLUTTER
SORRY...
IT'S NO PROBLEM.
SO, YOU OKAY?
YAAY
YAAH
AFTER THAT TIME...
YOU JUST LEFT IMMEDI-ATELY...
SO...
OH...

YEAH.
I'M FINE.
GOOD.
IS YOUR MOTHER DOING WELL?
OH... YEAH.
YOU'VE GOT TO CHEER UP!
OR SHE'LL WORRY ABOUT YOU...
ドキン
PANG...
I'M SORRY...
LISE...
YOU'RE SO KIND.
HUH?
WHAT ARE YOU SAYING?
くすくす
CHUCKLE CHUCKLE
バサッ
FLAP

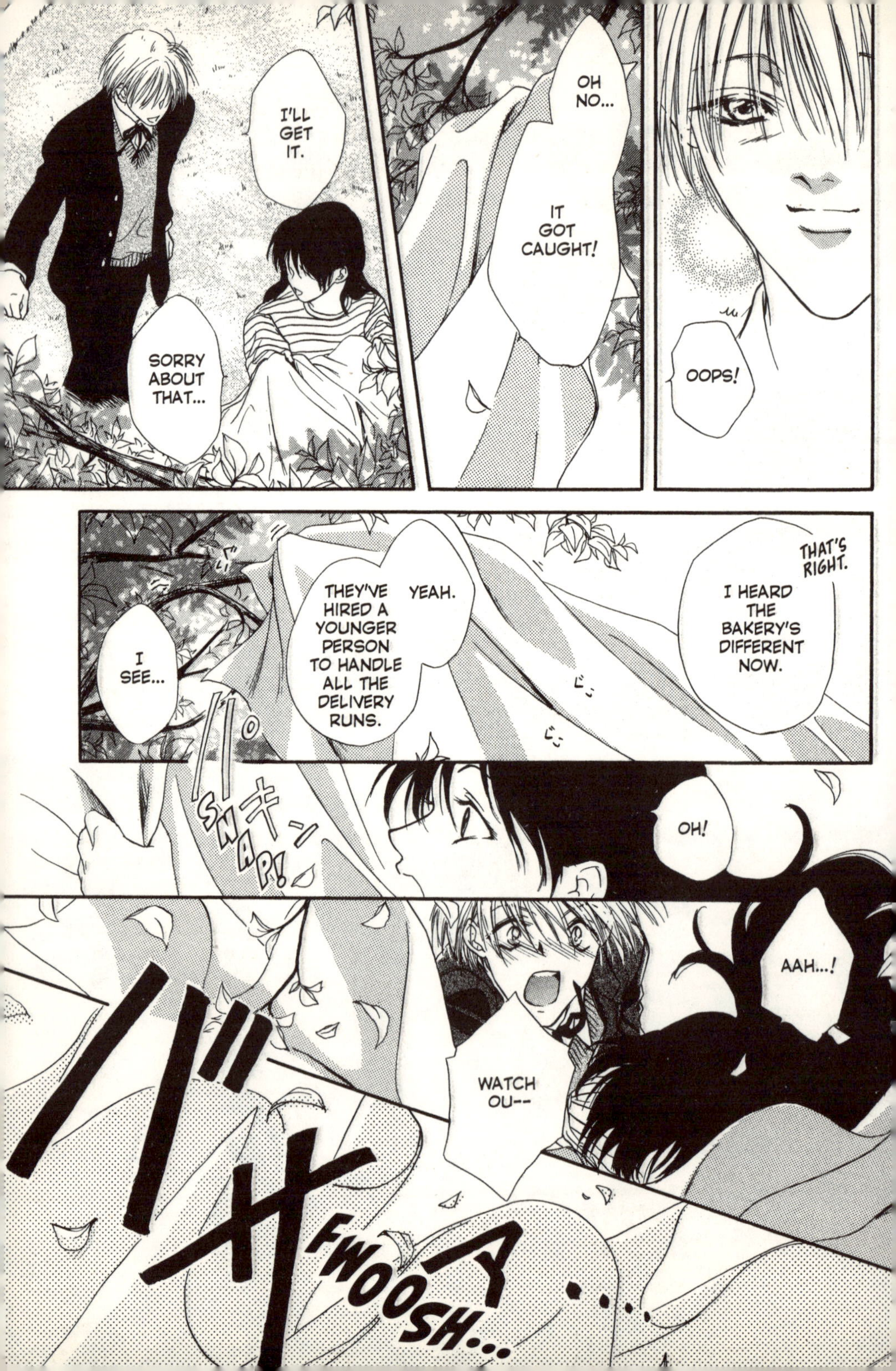
OOPS!
OH NO...
IT GOT CAUGHT!
I'LL GET IT.
SORRY ABOUT THAT...
THAT'S RIGHT.
I HEARD THE BAKERY'S DIFFERENT NOW.
YEAH.
THEY'VE HIRED A YOUNGER PERSON TO HANDLE ALL THE DELIVERY RUNS.
I SEE...
OH!
SNAP!
AAH...!
WATCH OU--
FWOOSH...

NNN...
フア
FLUTTER...
ぱっ
WHISH
OW...
SORRY... ARE YOU OKAY?
OOOHH...
YEAH, I'M OK...
ゴト
CLUNK
AAAAHHH!

WHY YOU ...!!
DA
DA
AAH ...!
DA
DA
DA
DA
SMASH

THE PRINCIPAL'S OFFICE.
学園長室。
OH!
ALL I DID WAS REACH UP...
CLATTER
WOBBLE
CRASH
HOW DID IT HAPPEN?
CONVINCED.
YUP!
THIS WAS AN ACCIDENT.
NOT MY FAULT.
FLAP...
C...
CORAL...

ALAIN...
SO HE LIVES IN THE DORMS...
AND THE DORM RULES ARE STRICT...
AT ANY RATE,
HE'S ON CAMPUS...
"ARE YOU DRAWN TO THE WHITENESS AGAIN?"
BA-THUMP... ドクン
BA-THUMP... ドクン
BA-THUMP... ドクン

GU...
CLANG...
MORNING!
GOOD MORNING!
MORNIN'...
HM...
MORNING.
YAAY!
MORNING, GEORGES!
OH!
GOOD MORNING.

WHIP
E...
SNAP
ぐぎっ
?!
YOU...
WHA...
THWAP
WH- WHAT?! THAT HURT!

YOU...
THAT...
WHAT HAPPENED?
HUH?
OH...
HEE HEE!
AN ACCIDENT.
THERE WAS A LITTLE MISUNDER-STANDING YESTERDAY...
THE BAKER HIT ME.
REALLY?
YEAH ...?
I SEE...
WHEW...
IT'S NO USE...
NO...
TELL ME IF ANYTHING HAPPENS TO YOU.
PEOPLE OF THE ARGENT FAMILY
?!
SMACK
SIGH...
...I...
"DON'T GET CLOSE ...!"
HUH?

SO, YOU'VE FINALLY SHOWN YOUR TRUE COLORS, YOU ROGUE!!
STAND DOWN!
GRRR
WHY YOU LITTLE...
YOU'VE BEGUN ATTACKING ME NOW, HAVE YOU?
DON'T, YOU GUYS, DON'T!
HEH
DOOOOM
OVER AND OVER, ALL THE RUCKUS YOU CAUSE--
I COMPLIMENT YOU ON YOUR AIM, HOWEVER.
HUH!
I'M GOING TO TEACH YOU A LESSON.
GET BACK HERE, YOU RUNT!
AAAAAHHH!
BWA HA HA!
OHH, THAT STUPID SIR FREDDY.
BWA HA HA!
HE'S A LOVABLE FOOL!
BWA HA HA!
SLUMP
OHH...
CLUNK
SHEESH...
YOU CAN'T TRUST HIM FOR ONE SECOND...
WHY A CHAIR?
THAT JERK...
PAF
PAF

YOU'VE BEEN LETTING YOUR GUARD DOWN LATELY.
YOU'VE EVEN GOT A BRUISE...
HUH?
MY GUARD?
WHERE?
SORRY...
WHY ASK ME ...?
NOT THAT IT ISN'T FUN TO WATCH...
IN A WAY...
AS LONG AS I CAN SEE YOU'RE HAVING FUN, IT'S FINE WITH ME.
LITTLE BY LITTLE...
...I FEEL MORE AT EASE.
I REALLY...
...LIKE THIS PLACE...
WHAT?
NOTHING.

OH,
HOW'S YOUR MOM DOING?
SHE'S BEEN DOING REALLY WELL LATELY, THANKS TO YOU.
I SEE.
I'M GLAD. I HOPE SHE CONTINUES TO RECOVER.
YEAH... THANKS.
I'M SO GLAD YOUR FATHER'S OUR DOCTOR.
WHAT-EVER, AS LONG AS HE'S USEFUL TO YOU.
HENRI!
......
YOU AREN'T GOING TO BECOME A DOCTOR, HENRI?
EH.
IT DOESN'T INTEREST ME.
I SEE...
WHAT ABOUT YOU?
HUH ...?

I'M ASKING YOU THE SAME QUESTION.
WHAT DO YOU WANT TO BE?
I...
I'M NOT A SAINT, BUT...
I CAN STILL PLAY THE PIANO AS A CLERGYMAN, RIGHT...?
HUH?
ARE YOU SERIOUS?
CHUCKLE
I DON'T KNOW.
WELL...
I GUESS IT WOULD SUIT YOU.
NNN
ABOUT ME, THOUGH...
...I DON'T REALLY KNOW WHAT THE FUTURE HOLDS.

YOU'RE RIGHT...
BUT THE TRUTH IS...
I FEEL SO COMFORT-ABLE HERE...
THE PRE-SENT...
THE PEOPLE HERE... I LOVE THEM ALL.
I WISH THAT EVERYTHING COULD STAY THE SAME...
...WITH-OUT EVER CHANG-ING...
MURMUR ざわ
SORRY FOR DRAGGING YOU ALONG.
MURMUR ざわ
MURMUR ざわ

IS YOUR WOUND OKAY?
YEAH. SEE? IT'S HEALING ALREADY.
WHOA...
SORRY ABOUT THIS.
THIS WILL BE THE LAST SHOP.
カララン
TINKLE
WAIT FOR ME. I'LL BE RIGHT OUT!
YOU WERE IN THE MIDDLE OF DELIVERIES, WEREN'T YOU? SORRY TO HAVE TROUBLED YOU.
NO PROB-LEM.
I WAS ALMOST DONE ANYWAY. I'M GLAD YOU FOUND YOUR WALLET, THOUGH.
OH?
この
THIS VOICE...
THANK YOU!
NO PROB...
HEY!
THAT BLONDE HAIR!!! THAT UNIFORM!!!
ぎくぅ
FLINCH!
SLIGHT ATTEMPT TO GET AWAY.
I'M REALLY, REALLY SORRY!!!

OOOOH...
I REALLY THOUGHT LISE WAS BEING ATTACKED...
BECAUSE SHE'S SO CUTE!
HA OHHHHH...
NOISY!
HA
UM...
HA
IT'S OKAY...
HA
REALLY... THAT'S ENOUGH...
LOOK, IT'S ARTHUR!
IT'S ARTHUR AGAIN.
HA!
I MEAN, IF I'D *REALLY* LOOKED, I WOULD'VE NOTICED HOW WIMPY YOU ARE...
NO, REALLY...
HOW RUDE!
NEVER OCCURRED TO ME!
I PULLED MY PUNCH AT THE LAST SECOND, BUT I NEVER THOUGHT YOU WOULD FAINT...
I WASN'T EXPECTING THAT...
BLUSH
AAAAH!
PLEASE DON'T TALK ABOUT THAT!
ARTHUR-- HELPING A LITTLE BOY THIS TIME?
WHAT'S HE ASKING YOU?
ぎゃはは BWA HA HA
THAT'S NOT IT!
GO BACK TO STUDYING, STUDENT!
TEE HEE!
TRY NOT TO WEAR YOURSELF OUT WITH ALL YOUR ASSISTING!
MRRGH!
UH...
IT SEEMS LIKE YOU KNOW A LOT OF PEOPLE.
WELL, I MAKE A LOT OF DETOURS, SO...
?
BY THE WAY...
...WHAT'S YOUR RELATIONSHIP WITH LISE?
ZOOM
WHA?
WHAP
WHOA!
HEY!

ARE YOU AT IT AGAIN?!
WHOA!
IF YOU EVER LAY ANOTHER HAND ON THIS BOY, YOU'RE BANNED FROM THE ORPHAN-AGE!!
LISE!
HUH?
WHAT?
WHY ARE YOU WITH HIM?
HE'S HELPING ME WITH MY SHOPPING.
LET'S GO, LET'S GO.
WHAT?!
BUT I CAN HELP YOU WITH THAT!
......
YOU'RE IN THE MIDDLE OF WORK, AREN'T YOU?
YOU LEFT YOUR CAR OVER THERE.
LET ME GUESS-- YOU WERE HIJACKED BY SOME-ONE NEEDING HELP.
THE OWNER WILL YELL AT YOU AGAIN.
I DON'T CARE. I'LL DO ANYTHING YOU ASK ME TO, LISE.
THAT'S NOT...
AR-THUR!

DELIVERY VAN! ESCARGOT!
THE "ESCARGOT" WAS PARKED OVER THERE.
I KNEW YOU'D BE HERE!
HA HA! YOU WERE RIGHT!
THAT APRON SUITS YOU.
EMMA... LUCY...
GOOD TIMING! WE JUST BOUGHT THIS TINY LITTLE CLOTHES CHEST, BUT IT'S ACTUALLY KINDA HEAVY...
COULD YOU HELP US OUT?
OH...
BUT I'VE GOT ONE MORE DELIVERY TO MAKE...
WOW, HE'S REALLY DEPENDED-UPON.
WHAAAAT?
COME ON! PLEASE?!
HMM.
FINE, I'LL GO WITH YOU.
OKAY.
REALLY?
I KNEW I COULD RELY ON YOU!
YAAAY
OH.
SORRY, LISE. MAYBE NEXT TIME...

HUH?
GONE...
UM...
LISE ...?
たっ TAP
たっ TAP
たっ TAP
たっ TAP
I THINK THAT MAN IS IN LOVE WITH Y--
DON'T MAKE ME LAUGH!
WHOA!
HE'S COMPLETELY THOUGHTLESS. HE PUTS ON A GOOD FACE FOR EVERY-BODY.
EVEN DITCHING HIS WORK...
MAYBE... HE JUST CAN'T ABANDON PEOPLE IN NEED...?
HE SAYS THE SAME TYPE OF THING TO EVERYONE!
HE EVEN HURT YOU OUT OF IMPULSIVE-NESS.
HUH...?
ザワ STIR...
BUT... IT'S NOT LIKE HE DID IT ON-PURPOSE... HE WAS WORRIED...
ABOU-T...
SOMEHOW...
TUG
YOU ...!

ARE YOU LISTENING?
HE HURT YOU.
OUT OF HIS OWN SELFISH MISUNDERSTANDING.
YOU... MY PRECIOUS GEORGES!
BA-THUMP!
THAT'S ENOUGH!
THUMP
YOU DON'T HAVE TO STAND UP FOR HIM.
LET'S GO.
CLANG...
HEH HEH HEH! GEORGES!
WIGGLE
WIGGLE
WIGGLE
FLINCH!
HUH?!

HEH!
WE SAW YOU YESTERDAY!
...WITH AN OLDER WOMAN!
HEH HEH HEH
YEAH, YEAH!
HUH?
OH...
YOU MEAN LISE?
WHAT ?!
A WOMAN ?!
GRR!
CLATTER
GEORGES ?! WITH A WOMAN ?!
CLATTER
CLATTER
CLATTER
WHY ?!
WHAAAAT?!
NO FAIR!
WHA... WAIT...
WHAT ARE YOU SAYING...
WHHYY ?!
WAAH!
NO WAAAAY!
ALL FRIENDLY AND LOVEY-DOVEY...
RIGHT?
WAAH
YUP!
YEAH...
N...!
LISE IS A TEACHER AT THE ORPHANAGE AND...
SO, HER NAME IS LISE!
LUCKY DOG!
HUH?
WHAAAAT?!
I WON'T ALLOW IT!
I WON'T!
COME BACK TO US!!!
IT'S NOT FAIR!!
ARRGH!
THAT'S NOT IT!
RRGH!
WAAH
WAAH
WAAH
SO NOISY...
WAAH
FIRST THING IN THE MORNING, TOO.
WAAH
WAAH
WAAH
WHAT IS IT NOW ...?
NOOOOOO!
WAAH
HUH?
WAAH
WAAH!
WAAH
WAAH
HMPH!
GEORGES HAS A GIRL...
WHAT'S WITH THAT LOOK?
CLATTER
WAAH
WHA?
OH!
YAY!
ROBERT! IT'S ROBERT!!
SIR ROBERT--
WAAH!

HEY, HEY!
SPARKLE
SPARKLE
ALL EXCITED...
YOUR PREVIOUS SCHOOL WAS CO-ED, WASN'T IT?!
SWARM
KINDA HYPER...
TELL US!
YOU HAD A GIRL-FRIEND, DIDN'T YOU?!
HEY!
SWARM
FEELING KINSHIP...
ROBERT-- YOU'RE OLDER THAN US, AREN'T YOU?!
TELL US!
SQUEAL ♥ ?
SWARM
WHOA, ANNOYING!
HUH --?
SHUT UP AND LET ME SLEEP.
KICKED THE HABIT.
I DON'T CARE ABOUT STORIES ANYMORE.
SIGH...
"STORIES"?!
OOHHH...
TH...
THAT JUST ADDS INSULT TO INJURY...
WHEN HERE WE ARE, STUCK IN AN ALL-BOY'S SCHOOL LIKE THIS.
PLUS, I EVEN LIVE ON-CAMPUS!
AND ENCOUNTERS WITH GIRLS ARE CLOSE TO NIL!
I'M JEAN-- REMEMBER ME, EVERY-ONE...?

MAYBE I'LL START VOLUNTEER WORK OR SOMETHING, TOO.
RIGHT?
JUST ON WEEK-ENDS.
SPARKLE
WHAT? WHAT?
NOT WITH INTENTIONS LIKE YOURS.
HE HE HE!
OK, OK!
WELL, I'M SURE THERE'S TWO SIDES TO THE STORY, BUT...
FOR NOW, LET'S JUST SAY...
THUMP
ERWIN!!
GEORGES HAS GOT A GIRL-FRIEND.
LETS US REJOICE IN ANOTHER'S HAPPINESS.
CELEBRATE!
DOESN'T CARE AS LONG AS IT'S ENTERTAINING TO HIM.
WAAAH
WHY?!
DAM-MIT!
WHY SHOULD WE CELE-BRATE?!
STUPID!
SURE, IT'S FINE FOR YOU!
WAAAH
I TOLD YOU!
IT'S NOT TRUE!!
BLUSH!
I CAN'T SLEEP HERE.
TCH!
CLATTER
WAAH
WAAH
YOU GUYS ...!
HA!
BLUSH...
IT...

BLUSH...
カァ…
IT'S NOT TRUE!! OK?!
WHAT ARE YOU TELLING ME FOR?
DUMMY!
SMACK ぺちん
EEP!
HEEEY...
I'M NOT EMBARRASSED!!
MURMUR ざわ
DON'T BE EMBARRASSED
HEE HEE!
TEE
MURMUR ざわ
MURMUR ざわ
TIRED...
KCHAK
ガチャ

HOW'S HE DOING ...?
CLAK

CLAK
CLAK
CLAK
HAH!
HEY YOU!!
DON'T CLIMB THAT THING!! GET DOWN!
TAP
TAP
GAH!
YES, SIR--
DAR
KIDS THESE DAYS...
HEH...

CLAK...
HA HA!
G...
CLAK...
CLAK...
LISE!
TODAY'S NOT A DELIVERY DAY.
IT'S OK. IS THERE ANYTHING I CAN HELP YOU WITH?
I'LL DO ANY-THING.
NO.
BLUNT!

ガックリ
DOOOOM
LISE...
IT'S OK! JUST LEAVE HIM.
はっ
HUH!
WHAT...
EH? ALL THE TIME...
WHY ARE YOU ALWAYS HERE?
HUH...?
WHY ...?
NO PARTICULAR...
ずい。
ZOOM
WHAT ARE YOU DOING ?!
DON'T TOUCH HIM!
カゴン
BWAM
OWW!
IF YOU'VE GOT THE TIME TO BE HANGING AROUND HERE...
WHY DON'T YOU GO BACK AND LEARN HOW TO BAKE SOME GOOD BREAD?
DON'T BULLY BIG BROTHER!
TAKE THAT!
AND THAT!
GRR...
OW!!
OW OW
DIDN'T YOU WANT TO HAVE YOUR OWN SHOP?
... ...

LISE...
YOU REMEMBERED THAT?
I ONLY MENTIONED IT ONCE, IN PASSING...
AND TO THE SISTER, AT THAT.
カァ...
BLUSH...
IT'S BECAUSE...
ばっ
WHOOSH
OH! THAT'S RIGHT!
ガチャ
CHAK
I FORGOT!
I HAVE A PRESENT FOR YOU!
HA HA HA,
STUPID ME.
HERE!
MY SPECIALLY MADE LISE BREAD"!
SQUEAL
INSIDE IS LISE'S FAVORITE RASPBERRY JAM.
じゃじゃん
TA-DAAH
ガァン
SHOCK!
SIGH...
YOU SURE HAVE TIME ON YOUR HANDS...

OHHH...
I'VE GOT OTHER CHORES TO DO. SEE YOU.
BREAD!
WHY DON'T YOU GIVE UP AL-READY?
NOT A SPARK OF HOPE.
YUP...
FORGET IT.
YOU KIDS...
HEH HEH!
SIGH...
I LOVE HER SO MUCH...
I WONDER WHY IT DOESN'T GET THROUGH TO HER...
THUMP
パタン
YOU SEE...
I WANT TO HAVE MY OWN STORE ONE DAY.

THE KIND OF PLACE WHERE PEOPLE CAN HAVE A LEISURELY CONVERSATION...
...RELAXING AND...
...COMFORTABLE.
OH, HOW NICE!
THEN HOW ABOUT TAKING LESS CARE OF OTHER PEOPLE AND...
...CONCENTRATING ON YOUR OWN WORK?!
OW!
SIGH
ARTHUR!
BYE BYE!
OKAY THEN.
YOU HAVE FRIDAY OFF, DON'T YOU?

THE BACKYARD WALL NEEDS REPAINTING.
IT'S PRETTY HIGH IN SOME PLACES-- CAN YOU HELP ME? WITH THAT?
I...
IF YOU CAN'T, I UNDERSTAND.
REALLY.
I'LL BE HERE, I'LL BE HERE!
I'LL DEFINITELY BE HERE!
OHHH...
NO MATTER WHAT!
EVEN IF I'M CALLED IN TO WORK, I'LL BE HERE!!
THAT'S NO GOOD.
CHUCKLE...
TWO O'CLOCK, THEN.
GIGGLE GIGGLE!
YOU KNOW WHAT?
MARIE THINKS THE TEACHER LIKES ARTHUR, TOO.

I SEE...
MURMUR
MURMUR
MURMUR
FRIDAY
THAT'S RIGHT. NOW ALL YOU HAVE TO DO IS GO STRAIGHT DOWN THIS ROAD.
BE CAREFUL NOW.
THANK YOU-- YOU'VE BEEN A GREAT HELP.
BYE!
OHH...
I'M GLAD I LEFT EARLY.
OKAY!
I'M GONNA PAINT ME A WALL!
AHH!
B-BUMP
WHOA!

EMMA? WHAT ARE YOU DOING HERE?
OH!
ARTHUR!!
GRAB
がば
OH, GOOD!
I'M SO *GLAD* I RAN INTO YOU!!
WHAT'S WRONG?
I MISTAKENLY TOOK SOME IMPORTANT PAPERS FROM MY PART-TIME JOB HOME WITH ME.
AND NOW I'VE LEFT THE WHOLE ENVELOPE SOME-WHERE!
PLEASE HELP ME LOOK FOR IT!
HUH?
BUT... TODAY I'VE GOT OTHER...
CAN'T YOU CALL LUCY?
NO.
SHE'S GONE HOME TO SEE HER PARENTS.
I STOPPED BY SO MANY PLACES TODAY...
I'LL NEVER FIND IT ON MY OWN!

IF I DON'T FIND IT BY FIVE O'CLOCK, I'LL BE FIRED!
PLEASE, HELP ME!!
...OKAY.
BEEP...
......
MURMUR
MURMUR

TA...
HUH?
HE NEVER CAME?
YEAH.
NEVER-MIND. THAT'S HOW HE IS.

HE MUST HAVE HAD...
...SOME REASON?
PANG...
HE COULD'VE CALLED, AT LEAST.
LISE...
DID YOU MAKE ALL THIS?
HE MENTIONED SOMETHING ABOUT TODAY BEING HIS BIRTHDAY, SO...
HEY, YOU GUYS!
SORRY FOR THE WAIT.
ARTHUR CAN'T COME, SO YOU CAN ALL START EATING NOW.
YAAAY
わあっ
MAT-THEW...
SISTER WILL BE HERE SOON, SO LOOK AFTER THE PLACE WITH GEORGES, OKAY?
OKAY.
YAH
YAH
EEK
HEY WAIT!

ARE YOU GOING SOME-WHERE?
TO GET PAINT.
I WAS GOING TO ASK ARTHUR, BUT...
WELL,
I'LL COME WITH YOU.
THANKS.
PANG...
CLANK...
CLANK...
MURMUR
MURMUR
CLANK...

OH...
UH, I'M SORRY.
YOU'D BETTER BE GETTING HOME SOON.
HEY
LISE...
は HAH!
LISE... ABOUT ARTHUR...
NO... IT'S NOT ABOUT THAT.
THANK YOU, ARTHUR !!
SORRY TO MAKE YOU COME ALL THE WAY DOWN TO WORK WITH ME.
I'M JUST GLAD WE MANAGED TO FIND IT.

WHEW! NOW I WON'T HAVE TO QUIT COLLEGE!
COME ON--I'LL TREAT YOU TO SOME-THING!
UH...
NO, THAT'S OK.
WHAT? DON'T BE SO MODEST!
NO.
REALLY, I HAVE OTHER PLANS.
REALLY? I DIDN'T KNOW.
NOW I FEEL BAD...
IT'S OKAY.
YOU SURE ARE A NICE GUY!
WELL THEN...
LET'S GO.
LI...
HERE'S YOUR REWARD.
TUG
HUH ...?

ゴト
CLUNK!

WAITING FOR HIS SCENE.

DASH
LISE!

LISE ?!
WHIRL
だっ
WAI--
WHIP
ばっ

WHAT THE?! GET OUT OF MY WAY!
I WON'T!
WHA...
ARE YOU REALLY IN LOVE WITH LISE?
WHAT ARE YOU TALKING AB--
I FEEL...
THE TABLE WAS PILED WITH FOOD AND TREATS THAT LISE MADE.
...A CLAMORING IN MY HEART...
I HEAR IT'S YOUR BIRTHDAY TODAY.
!

OH...
NO WAY...
SHE WAS WAITING ALL DAY.
YOU PROMISED HER.
WHAT WERE YOU DOING?
WH...
THAT'S...
HEY,
WHAT IS THIS?
I DON'T WANNA BE INVOLVED IN SOME MESS!
I'VE GOT NOTHING TO DO WITH THIS!
HEY, YOU...
ALL ARTHUR DID WAS HELP ME OUT WHEN I WAS IN TROUBLE.
DON'T BLAME HIM.
FORGET IT.
ENOUGH...
THIS GUY JUST *CAN'T* REFUSE WHEN SOMEONE ASKS SOME-THING OF HIM.
THAT'S WHY WE ALWAYS END UP DEPENDING ON HIM...
HE'S A REALLY GOOD GUY, YOU KNOW?

OK?
PLEASE FORGIVE HIM.
IT... ISN'T FAIR SOMEHOW...
WHAT ...?
ACTING LIKE THAT!
BEING KIND TO EVERY-BODY!
LISE WAS...
HUH ...?
JOLT...
I JUST...
...WHO KNOWS MY PAST.
SHE'S THE ONLY ONE.
THE SINGLE PERSON...
I JUST WANT TO SEE THAT LISE IS ALWAYS SMILING.
BLUSH
ARE YOU IN LOVE WITH HER, TOO?
N...

THAT'S HOW I FEEL, TOO!
BUT!
OH... WHY DO I FEEL...
WATCHING YOU, IT SEEMS LIKE YOU TREAT THEM ALL THE SAME!
...THIS TROUBLED STIRRING IN MY HEART...
BOTH LISE AND THIS LADY...
THAT'S...
THAT'S NOT FAIR!
TO LISE...
"BEING THE SAME TO EVERYBODY..."

"IT'S ACTUALLY PRETTY CRUEL..."
PAN
OH...
I FEEL SORRY...
FOR LISE...
TH...
I NEVER...
SO THAT'S WHY...
I GET IT NOW...
I NEVER MEANT...

THIS PERSON...
I NEVER MEANT IT TO BE THAT WAY.
IS ME...
PANG
"HE'S COMPLETELY THOUGHTLESS."
IF...
LISE...
CLENCH...
PAN...
...IS REALLY THE ONE MOST IMPORTANT TO YOU...
"HE SAYS THE SAME TYPE OF THING TO EVERYBODY..."

PLEASE. DON'T DO WHAT YOU DID TODAY, EVER AGAIN...
BEING TOO KIND...
IF YOU CAN'T DO THAT...
...CAN END UP HURTING SOMEONE.
...PLEASE DON'T SAY ANYTHING TO GET LISE'S HOPES
UP...

MR. ARTHUR!
WAI...
BE QUIET!
I'M GOING TO SEE LISE!
I HAVE TO APOLOGIZE TO HER!

I DON'T CARE WHAT YOU SAY...
I LOVE LISE!!
SHE'S MY NUMBER-ONE!!
WHOAA!
NUMBER-ONE...

LISE--!!!
びくっ
JUMP
WHAT?
ARTHUR?!
ぶはっ
BFFT!
I'M SORRY ABOUT TODAY!
IT WAS COMPLETELY MY FAULT!!
BLUSH
IT'S ARTHUR!!
BUT BELIEVE ME!
I REALLY LOVE YOU THE MOST!
BECAUSE...!

WHEN I GET YELLED AT BY THE OWNER FOR TAKING TOO MANY DETOURS...
YOU'RE THE ONLY ONE WHO'S CONCERNED FOR ME!
I KNOW...
I KNOW THAT IT'S A BAD HABIT OF MINE TO WORRY OVER OTHER PEOPLE.
BUT,
IF IT MAKES YOU FEEL THAT BADLY,
I WON'T LISTEN TO OTHER PEOPLE'S REQUESTS ANYMORE.
NO MATTER WHAT...
NO MATTER WHO'S IN TROUBLE...
CLENCH
I'LL COME STRAIGHT DOWN HERE...
HUH?
YOU FOOL!

IF YOU EVER BECOME LIKE THAT...
...I'LL HATE YOU.
AWWWW...
GRIN
HUH?
HURRY UP AND COME INSIDE-- THIS IS SO EMBARRASSING!
ARTHUR !!!

きゃ YAAAAY っ...
OH, MY.
HERE.
I TOOK IT HOME WITH ME.
ガチャ CLANK...

I'M SORRY...
...YOU GOT CAUGHT UP IN ALL THIS...
IT'S OKAY.
I'M REALLY SORRY.
IT'S OKAY!
YAAAH
YAAAY!
I'M SORRY...
PAN...
YOU LOVE HIM, HUH?
MM...
CLANK...
IT'S JUST THAT I WANT TO BE TREASURED BY THE ONE THAT *I* TREASURE.

HE'S ALL MUDDLED. HE LIVES ON IMPULSE....
HE'S THOUGHTLESS... HE'S THE SAME TO EVERYONE...
BUT HE'S ALSO KIND TO EVERYONE...
WHEN SOMEONE ASKS HIM FOR HELP, HE CAN'T REFUSE...
THAT'S WHAT I LOVE ABOUT HIM.
BUT EVEN SO...
I STILL WANT HIM TO SEE ONLY ME.
IT ISN'T FAIR, IS IT?
THAT'S NOT TRUE.

REALLY?
YEAH.
DO YOU THINK THAT WAY, TOO?
I'M...
FINE...
I'M FINE WITH THE WAY I AM...
WHAT IF
SOME-BODY...
...WANTED YOU? WHAT WOULD YOU DO?
WHAT IF THEY WANTED YOU,
AND NO ONE ELSE?
ドキ
JOLT...
TH...

THAT...
STUPID AND NAIVE...
UNBEARABLY WEAK...
I'M NO GOOD...
I KNOW THAT...
...WILL NEVER HAPPEN.
I COULDN'T DO IT.
I COULD NEVER TREAT EVERYONE THE SAME.
IN THE END, I'LL CHOOSE SOMEONE SPECIAL.
AND...
...IF I FEEL 100% ABOUT SOME-ONE,
I'D WANT THE OTHER PERSON TO THINK 100% OF ME, TOO.

IF THAT PERSON IS PRECIOUS TO ME, THEN ALL THE MORE REASON.
I KNOW IT CAN'T BE THAT WAY ALL THE TIME.
I KNOW THAT.
BUT...
...WHEN THE OTHER PERSON LOVES YOU BACK JUST AS MUCH AS YOU LOVE HIM...
...THAT'S THE HAPPIEST FEELING IN THE WORLD...

OH.
SORRY.
DID THAT MAKE *ANY* SENSE?
SURE IT DID.
I THINK I UNDER-STAND...
IT'S JUST THAT I'VE NEVER EXPERI-ENCED...
...SOME-THING LIKE THAT.
YOU WILL.
SOMEDAY.

WHEN A "FAVORITE" IS BORN IN HERE.
FAVORITE...

IF SUCH A DAY...
YEAH...
EVER COMES...
"FAVORITE"
OH! I KNOW! IT'S MY MOM!
WHAA...
カラ
CLANG...
ざわ
CHATTER
ざわ
CHATTER
YOU DUMMY
I TOLD YOU SO!
AWW, HOW DISAP-POINTING.
ざわ
CHATTER
OH YOU GUYS...
も
"HOW'S HE DOING ...?"

YOU ALWAYS SEEM TO KNOW THE ANSWER.
THIS BALD DUDE-- WHAT'S HIS NAME?
I'VE BEEN ASSIGNED TO HIM!
THIS ENGLISH LITERATURE GUY!
TELL ME SIMPLY, IN GREAT DETAIL!!
WHADDAYA MEAN "SIMPLY, IN GREAT DETAIL"?
HEY...
HEY...
ROBERT !!
HE'S DOING JUUUST FINE.
HMPH!
NAP TIME.
OH, MAN!
SO, IT WASN'T TRUE?
WHAT?
ARE YOU RELIEVED?
THAT WASN'T HIS GIRLFRIEND!
FOOL!
THAT'S NOT IT.
HOW BORING...
IT JUST SEEMED LIKE IT WOULD BE FUN TO TALK ABOUT.
ISN'T THERE ANYTHING FUN GOING ON?
OH!
SO THIS IS SHAKESPEARE!
AND HIS WORKS?
...I'M TIRED.

I'M LEAVING.
ガタ
CLATTER
ざわ CHATTER
HUH?
BUT IT'S ONLY SECOND PERIOD!
WHAT ABOUT MY SHAKE-SPEARE?!
ざわ CHATTER
ざわ CHATTER
カッ TAP...
NOTHING WILL CHANGE...
"NO ONE AROUND YOU...
...CAN REMAIN UNIN-VOLVED."
IT'S ALREADY OVER WITH...
NOTHING WILL RETURN...

"YOU'RE PROBABLY THE ONE"
"WHO CHOSE HIM-- RIGHT?"
DON'T THINK--
コツ… THUNK...
STOP ALL THOUGHT...
IT'S ALL
--SO USE-LESS...
AN ILLUSION...

カラーーン……
CLANG...
ざわ MURMUR
ざわ MURMUR
ざわ MURMUR
ざわ MURMUR
カラーーン……
CLANG...
--ERT...

YOU CAN'T SLEEP UP THERE.
LOUIS WILL SCOLD YOU AGAIN.
WAKE UP, ROBERT!
COME ON...
GR... A...
ROBERT!
CLAP

OH, I'M SO GLAD-- YOU SCARED ME!
WERE YOU JUST SLEEPING?
WHAT ARE YOU DOING?
WHY ARE YOU SITTING DOWN HERE?
I THOUGHT YOU FELL OUT OF THE TREE!
HA...
WHAT?
TOO MUCH SLEEP!
寝すぎ
CHUCKLE...
ARE YOU STILL IN A DAZE?
COME ON.
CLASS IS STARTING.
YOU SHOULDN'T DITCH JUST BECAUSE IT'S ENG--
--LISH...

ROBE--
BE QUIET...

CLANG...
BA-THUMP...
...LISTEN...
IT'S THE SUMMONING BELL...
CLANG...
JUST BE QUIET...
BA-THUMP...
BA-THUMP...
CLANG...
I MUST PROTECT...

JOLT
WHOOSH

The Summoning Bell ◆ END

DO YOU BELIEVE IN GOD, GRACE?
OF COURSE.
BECAUSE YOU DO, LOUIS.
BE-CAUSE...
IF WE HAVE FAITH, HE WILL CERTAINLY BRING HAPPINESS TO US ALL.
THAT'S WHY I LOVE HIM...
WHY I LOVE GOD...
I TRUST IN HIM.
HA HA!
IF YOU KEEP SAYING YOU LOVE HIM SO MUCH...
...GOD WILL...
...TAKE YOU AWAY.

WHOOSH
HUFF...
HUFF...
HUFF...
CREAK...
HUFF...

DAMN...
偶像
ICON

RRRRRRRING
SNAP
AAAAAHHHHH!!
NO WAY?!
BANG
CLATTER
STOMP
OW!
OH!
SORRY, DID I WAKE YOU?
CLATTER...
STOMP
GEORGES?
IT'S ALL RIGHT.
BUT...
I SET THE ALARM WRONG!
I'M SO STUPID...

OH, NO... IT WAS BECAUSE OF ME, WASN'T IT?
YOUR RIBBON IS CROOKED!
I'LL FIX IT LATER.
NO, THAT'S NOT IT.
NEVERMIND-- BE SURE TO STAY IN BED. I'LL BE BACK EARLY TODAY.
KCHAK ガチャ
BUT YOU HAVE PIANO LESSONS TODAY.
IT'S ALL RIGHT, I'LL TAKE THE DAY OFF.
SO STAY IN BED!
I'M OFF!
た... TA...
GOOD MORNING.
OH!
GOOD MORNING.
I'M OFF TO SCHOOL!
タン TAP
WHAT ARE YOU IN SUCH A HURRY FOR?
BE CAREFUL NOW!
タン TAP
タン TAP

SO FULL OF LIFE...
YES MA'AM!
GOOD MORNING, ANNE.
GOOD MORNING.
HOW UNUSUAL-- HE'S TARDY? DID HE STAY UP LATE OR SOME-THING?
I HAD A FEVER LAST NIGHT...
I SEE... SO CARING TOWARD HIS MOTHER. WHAT A GOOD BOY.
CHUCKLE!
HE'S SO OVER-PROTECTIVE...
TA...
HUFF...
CLANG...
OH!

OHHHH...
IT'S THE FINAL HYMN...
TARDY FOR THE FIRST TIME.
ガクー
SLUMP
OH, IT'S YOU.
ROBERT!
ばっ
WHIP
OH.
HOW UNUSUAL.
THAT'S NOT ...!
カァー
BLUSH
DON'T PUT ME IN THE SAME CATEGORY AS *YOU!*
たっ
TA...
SO, YOU'VE FINALLY STARTED CUTTING CLASS, TOO.
HE HE HE HE!
SO SLEEPY...
FWAAA...
あふ
F...
HUH?

CIRCLES UNDER HIS EYES ...?
WHAT IS IT?
YOU'VE...
BEEN NAPPING A LOT LATELY.
INSOMNIA?
OH...
IT'S THE SPRING WEATHER.
ACTUALLY...
IT'S ALMOST SUMMER...
THE ROSES ARE IN FULL BLOOM...
IT IS SUM-MER...
LATELY...
...HAVEN'T YOU BEEN...
ACTING A LITTLE STRANGE?
"JUST BE QUIET..."
TAP...
CHUCKLE!
OH DEAR.
WHO DO WE HAVE HERE, CUTTING CLASS?
HA...!

I...
MASS STARTED LONG AGO.
I'M SO SORRY!
WAAAAH!
IT'S ALL RIGHT... I'M NOT OFFICIAL STAFF HERE YET.
UM...
?
...ARE YOU OUR NEW PRIEST?
PEEK
ひょい
YES.
THERE'S A TEMPORARY ABSENCE AT THE CHAPEL, SO I WAS CALLED IN AS A REPLACEMENT.
PEEK
ひょい
?
I JUST TRANSFERRED TODAY.

HUH?
COME TO THINK OF IT, AT THE LAST MASS...
THERE WAS AN ANNOUNCE-MENT, RIGHT?
YES, YES.
SEE? THOSE WHO ATTEND ARE SUPPOSED TO KNOW ALL ABOUT IT.
WHIP
TCH!
RIGHT...
ROBERT?
I HAVEN'T HEARD ANYTHING ABOUT IT!
I NEVER HEARD THAT *YOU* WOULD BE COMING HERE!
LIKE I SAID, THOSE WHO ATTEND LIKE THEY'RE SUPPOSED TO...
HUH?
HUH?
HUH?
OH? DIDN'T FATHER MENTION IT?

UM...
ROBERT?
GLANCE...
!!
GAH!
YOU GO OVER THERE!
YAH! YAH!
SHOVE
HUH?!
WHA...
WHAT ARE YOU D...
SHOVE
SHOVE
WHAT'S GOING ON?
OH, MY...
A FRIEND OF YOURS, ROBERT?
OH!
TCH
YES!
HA...
AH...
I SEE...

NICE TO MEET YOU.
I'M ROBERT'S OLDER BROTHER, LOUIS FRANCISCO ONYX.
O...
HUH...
OLDER BROTHER !!
NICE TO MEET YOU!
I'M GEORGES SAPHIR!
OH, HOW CUTE.
HOW DO YOU DO.
I'M GLAD...
YOU SEEM WELL...
MR. SAPHIR.
JOLT!
YES!

PLEASE...
...BE A GOOD FRIEND TO ROBERT.
YES.
HEART-WARMING
WHA...!
TUG ぐい
WHOA!
WHAT ARE YOU TALKING ABOUT?!
WE'RE NOT LITTLE KIDS!
AND WHAT ARE YOU ANSWERING HIM FOR?
WHAT ARE YOU, STUPID?
HA HA HA!
HE'S EMBARRASSED.
CHUCKLE くす
CHUCKLE くす
CHUCKLE くす
LOUIS!
HUH?
BUT I... COULDN'T HELP IT...

...THAT THE NUMBER-ONE TROUBLEMAKER IS *ALSO* THE PRINCIPAL'S SON.
WE'RE GOING NOW! WE'VE GOT CLASS!
WHA ?! WHOSE LINE IS THAT ?!
SHUT UP!
YOW!
OH, THAT'S RIGHT.
I SAW FATHER EARLIER-- HE WAS VERY FRUS-TRATED...
SON ...?
WHAT ...?
WHAAAAT?!
IS THAT TRUE ?!
LOUIS !!
WHY YOU ...!
A HA HA HA!
CLANG
CLANG

BYE BYE!
カラーン…
CLANG...
ぐったり。
SLUMP
YEAH, SEE YOU.
SEE YOU.
BYE BYE.
A--
--RE YOU OKAY?
...NO.
SORRY.
IT'S ABOUT "THE PRINCIPAL'S SON" THING, RIGHT?
わ～ん
WAAAH...
I DIDN'T MEAN TO, BUT I JUST OVERHEARD...
I COULDN'T HELP IT.
WERE YOU HIDING IT OR SOMETHING?
NOT PARTICULARLY.
IT DIDN'T SEEM WORTH MENTIONING...
AND THEN HE JUST BLURTS IT OUT!
I DIDN'T KNOW YOU HAD A BROTHER... HOW MANY?
UMM...
TWO.
REALLY?! YOU'RE SO LUCKY!
ぱぁ…
GLOW
HOW SO?!
ガタ…
CLATTER...

SEE YOU, GEORGES!
I'M AN ONLY CHILD, SO I ENVY PEOPLE WITH SIBLINGS.
OH, BYE BYE.
YOU'RE JUST IDEALIZING.
ROLL
YEAH?
NO I'M NOT!
YEAH.
OH.
I'VE GOT TO GET HOME.
I PROMISED I'D PLAY THE PIANO.
ガチャ KCHAK
FOR WHO?
MY MOTHER.
...OEDI-PUS COM-PLEX.
カ BLUSH...
IT'S N--
ガス THUMP
THAT'S NOT IT!
MY MOTHER HAS A WEAK CONSTITU-TION...
THAT'S NOT IT!
ガスッ THUMP
SHE DOESN'T GO OUT MUCH OR ANY-THING...
THAT'S WHY...
PULSE...
DO YOU LOOK LIKE HER ...?

HUH?
UHH... LET'S SEE-- DO I?
I DON'T GET TOLD THAT TOO OFTEN... MAYBE BECAUSE I'M A BOY.
I DON'T KNOW.
HMM?
OH...
HEH...
I SEE...
SORRY.
CLAK
HUH? ABOUT WHAT?
THE "OEDIPUS COMPLEX."
YOU SEE...
HE'S ALWAYS SLEEPING THERE...

くす CHUCKLE
I'M SURE HE'S GOING TO GET FOUND OUT BY THE PRIEST SOON!
YOU MUST BE HAVING FUN.
HUH?
IT SHOWS ON YOUR FACE LATELY.
REA... LLY?
カ... BLUSH...
SCHOOL...
IT'S FUN?
HUH...?
I... GUESS...

ガタ
CLATTER
BUT!
IT'S ALWAYS BEEN FUN!
IT'S NOT JUST LATELY!
IT'S ALWAYS BEEN THE SAME.
CHUCKLE...
YOU'RE RIGHT.
HAS SHE FOUND ME OUT ...?
THAT I'VE BEEN TRYING NOT TO WORRY HER...
FORCING MYSELF TO PUT ON A HAPPY FACE.
NO MATTER WHAT...
... ...
WHICH WOULD YOU LIKE?
BACH?
SCHUBERT?

ガタ
THUD...
YOU LIKE...
GOUNOD'S *AVE MARIA*-- DON'T YOU, MOTHER.
ガタン
CLATTER
MOTHER?!
カチャ
CLINK
ムス…
MRGH...
カチャ
CLANK

SINCE YOU'RE DOWN HERE ANYWAY, I THOUGHT I'D INVITE YOU BUT...
WAS IT INCONVENIENT?
NO.
AS LONG AS I RETURN SOMETIME TODAY, IT'S FINE.
YOU'D BETTER SHOW UP, TOO.
I'M LOOKING FORWARD TO MASS TOMORROW.
WHAT ARE YOU DOING HERE?
HE FINDS YOU REALLY ENDEAR-ING.
CUT IT OUT-- IT'S CREEPY.
FA-THER...
GIGGLE...
CHUCKLE...
I SWEAR...
SOME-HOW...
YOU'VE CHANGED, FATHER.
...YOU WEREN'T LIKE THIS BEFORE.
IGNORE
WHAT'S WITH THE *ATTITUDE* ?!
SIR, YOU HAVE A PHONE CALL.
CHUCKLE!

I'M GLAD...
YOU SEEM TO BE DOING WELL, TOO.
......
THAT BOY...
WHAT WAS HIS NAME... SAPHIR?
TO BE PERFECTLY HONEST, I WAS SHOCKED.
HE'S THE EXACT IMAGE.
CHUCKLE...
I THOUGHT HE WAS A GIRL.
AND...
...I KNOW THIS SOUNDS FUNNY...
BUT THE FACT THAT YOU SEEMED OK AROUND HIM...
"YOU'RE SO LUCKY..."
...PUT MY MIND AT EASE.
PANG...

IT'S ALREADY BEEN TWO YEARS,
SINCE GRACE PASSED AWAY...
AT THE TIME OF THE ACCIDENT
I REALLY DIDN'T KNOW WHAT WOULD BECOME OF YOU...
STOP IT!
I DON'T WANT TO HEAR IT FROM YOU!
THE REASON GRACE WANTED TO BECOME A NUN...
IT'S NONE OF YOUR BUSI-NESS!
WE DON'T EVEN SHARE THE SAME BLOOD!
CLATTER
YOU DON'T UNDER-STAND AT ALL!
YOU PROBABLY HAVEN'T EVEN REALIZED WHY!

BAM
ROBERT !!
DAMN...
THUD
"YOU SEE..."
"GOD IS ALWAYS WATCHING OVER US."
IT'S A LIE...
"LOUIS SAID THAT?"
"YES..."
"I WANT TO BECOME A NUN."
IF THAT'S TRUE...
THEN WHY DOESN'T HE HELP US...
"I WANT TO BE LIKE LOUIS..."
G...

IN THE NAME OF OUR LORD.
JESUS CHRIST.
CHK...
チャリ…
AMEN.
RUSTLE...
ざわ…
MURMUR
ざわ
MURMUR
ざわ
MURMUR
ざわ
MURMUR
ざわ
OH...
WHEW...

TA...
GOOD MOR--
HMPH
WHAT...?
MURMUR
MURMUR
MURMUR
HUH ...?
GEORGES.
YOU WERE SPACING OUT DURING MASS.
WHAT'S WRONG?
CHATTER
OH...
IT WAS JUST A LITTLE STUFFY IN THERE AND...
CHATTER
DOES IT HAVE TO DO WITH YOUR MOM?
WHAT?

MY DAD LEFT THE HOUSE YESTERDAY ON A SUDDEN CALL, SO I THOUGHT IT MIGHT BE TO YOUR PLACE.
MURMUR
"THE PEOPLE OF THE ARGENT FAMILY"-- 2000 ECUS A COPY! A SPECIAL PRICE FOR FRIENDS!
THAT'S TOO EXPENSIVE, SIR FREDDY.
STOP HAWKING YOUR WARES, PRINCE.
MURMUR
MURMUR
NO, IT WASN'T ME.
REALLY?
YEAH. EVERY-THING'S FINE.
A TOP SECRET MISSION?
I SEE... DAD WON'T TELL ME ANYTHING.
HE COULD AT LEAST DENY IT.
WE'RE FINE... THANKS.
I'M SORRY...
TAP...
KCHAK...

OH.
SO, YOUR BROTHER STARTED TODAY.
HM.
EH... I WASN'T THERE.
I SEE...
UM...
UH
SORRY.
I'VE GOT OTHER THINGS TO DO.
カッ
TAP...
OH...
カッ
TAP
OK...
カッ
TAP
カッ...
TAP...
DAMN...
YOUR FEVER'S STILL A LITTLE HIGH.

SHALL I CALL THE DOCTOR?
NO, IT'S NOTHING...
THIS USED TO HAPPEN ALL THE TIME AFTER JACK DIED.
I'LL STAY HOME TODAY.
I'M FINE.
I'LL COME LOOK IN ON HER FROM TIME TO TIME.
BUT...
DON'T CRY...
I'LL PROTECT YOU...
KEEP SMILING...
COME NOW...
DON'T LOOK LIKE THAT.
"YOU MUST BE HAVING FUN..."
"IT SHOWS ON YOUR FACE LATELY..."
YOU GO ON TO SCHOOL.
OK?
WHAT IS THERE...

...THAT I CAN DO...?
OKAY.
CRUNCH...
ジャリ
JOLT!
ビクッ
ばっ
WHISH

ザッ
..ZSH...
バタ
SLAM...

THE PRIEST IS...
TAP...
コツ
CLAK

JESUS...
I BEG YOU...
MOTHER MARY...
チャリ… CHAK...
LISTEN TO MY PLEA...
O HEAVEN, HEAR MY PRAYER...
ギイ… CREAK...

CRK...
ROBERT...
...WHAT ARE YOU DOING?
OH!
TAP...
I WAS JUST SEEING IF THE FATHER WAS HERE...
LOUIS?
WHY?
HUH...?
STIR...
UM...
MY MOTHER'S NOT WELL...
SO, I CAME TO PRAY...
SHE'S BED-RIDDEN, BUT...
SHE INSISTS SHE'S OKAY...
I WANTED TO TALK TO THE FATHER ABOUT IT...
THAT'S WHY...

"IS LOUIS THE REASON FOR YOUR FAITH, GRACE?"
"NO, THAT'S NOT IT."
...THE FATHER WOULD LISTEN TO MY STORY.
AND I THOUGHT IT MIGHT EASE MY MIND...
"I MADE MY OWN CHOICE."
TAP...
BECAUSE...
THEN SAVE US!
BA-THUMP...
...OP...
IT'S NO USE...
PRAYING HERE...
BA-THUMP...
IT'S MEANING-LESS...
SAVE ...!!
...IS ALL I CAN DO...
STOP IT...
STOP IT...
BA-THUMP...

STOP IT!!

ROBE...
!!
WHAP
KSHAK
ROB-
ERT
!!
WHIP

バターン
SLAM

STOP IT!!
MR. SAPHIR?
WHAT IS WRONG?
YOU LOOK UPSET.

FATHER...
YOU CAN JUST CALL ME LOUIS.
MAY I SIT?
OH.
YES.
OH? IT'S BROKEN.
ER...
LET ME SEE... I CAN FIX IT.
OH?
WHAT PRETTY STONES.
OH.
MY PARENTS...
I'M TOLD THEY GAVE THAT TO ME WHEN I WAS BORN...TO PROTECT ME.
CHK...
I SEE...

YOU'RE VERY DEVOUT, AREN'T YOU?
CHAK
CHAK
UM...
YES?
BOTH YOU... AND THE PRINCIPAL...
SEEM VERY DEVOUT, TOO...
BUT...
ROBERT?
UH...
CHUCKLE!
HE HATES BOTH GOD AND ME, YOU KNOW.
CHAK
HATES...
I THINK HE'S NOT TOTALLY WITHOUT BELIEF.
FAITH IS UP TO THE INDIVIDUAL, AFTER ALL.
BE-CAUSE HE BE-LIEVED...
...HE CAN'T FOR-GIVE.
BUT I THINK IT'S PROBABLY...
...ALL MY FAULT...

WHAT?
THERE, IT'S FIXED.
HERE.
チャリ… CHAK…
THANK YOU VERY MUCH.
CRUNCH…
IF…
…SOMEONE SHOULD SAY SOMETHING TO YOU…
…AND YOU DON'T UNDER-STAND WHAT TO DO…
…WELL, ONE SHOULD FOLLOW ONE'S OWN BELIEFS.
THAT'S WHAT I THINK.
ガタ… CLATTER…
UM …!

MY MOTHER ...!
SHE'S NOT WELL...
BUT...
I...
ALL I CAN DO...
IS PRAY...
THUMP
IT'S OKAY. THAT'S FINE.
YOU DO WHAT YOU CAN DO.
I HOPE FOR YOUR MOTHER'S QUICK RECOVERY, TOO.
I'LL KEEP HER IN MY PRAYERS TO GOD.

OK?
OK.
I'LL LEAVE YOU THIS MEDICINE FOR YOUR FEVER.
IF THIS DOESN'T LOWER IT, THEN... I'LL BE CONCERNED.
I REALLY WISH YOU WOULD CHECK IN TO THE HOSPITAL.
DON'T BE SILLY.
HE'S NOT A LITTLE CHILD ANYMORE.

KNOCK KNOCK
YOU'RE RIGHT...
CHAK
DOCTOR?
OH...I'M LEAVING SOME MEDICINE HERE.
THANK YOU VERY MUCH.
SHE DOESN'T SEEM TO HAVE MUCH OF AN APPE-TITE,
BUT CRAM SOME FOOD DOWN HER GULLET TO MAKE HER EAT, WILL YOU?
HOW AWFUL!
HA HA...
HA HA...
WELL THEN, I'LL BE OFF.
TAKE CARE.
THUNK

SORRY TO WORRY YOU.
CLAK
IT'S OKAY.
EVERY-THING'S FINE...
YES.

WHY ...?
YOU KNOW, DON'T YOU ...?
"WITH LOUIS, I'M NOT SCARED."
"I'M AT EASE..."
"IF YOU HAVE FAITH AND PRAY FOR HAPPI-NESS"
"EVEN ALL THE BAD THINGS--"
"YOU'LL BE ABLE TO FORGET..."
SEE...
THAT'S WRONG...
"LOUIS SAID..."
YOU KNOW ...!

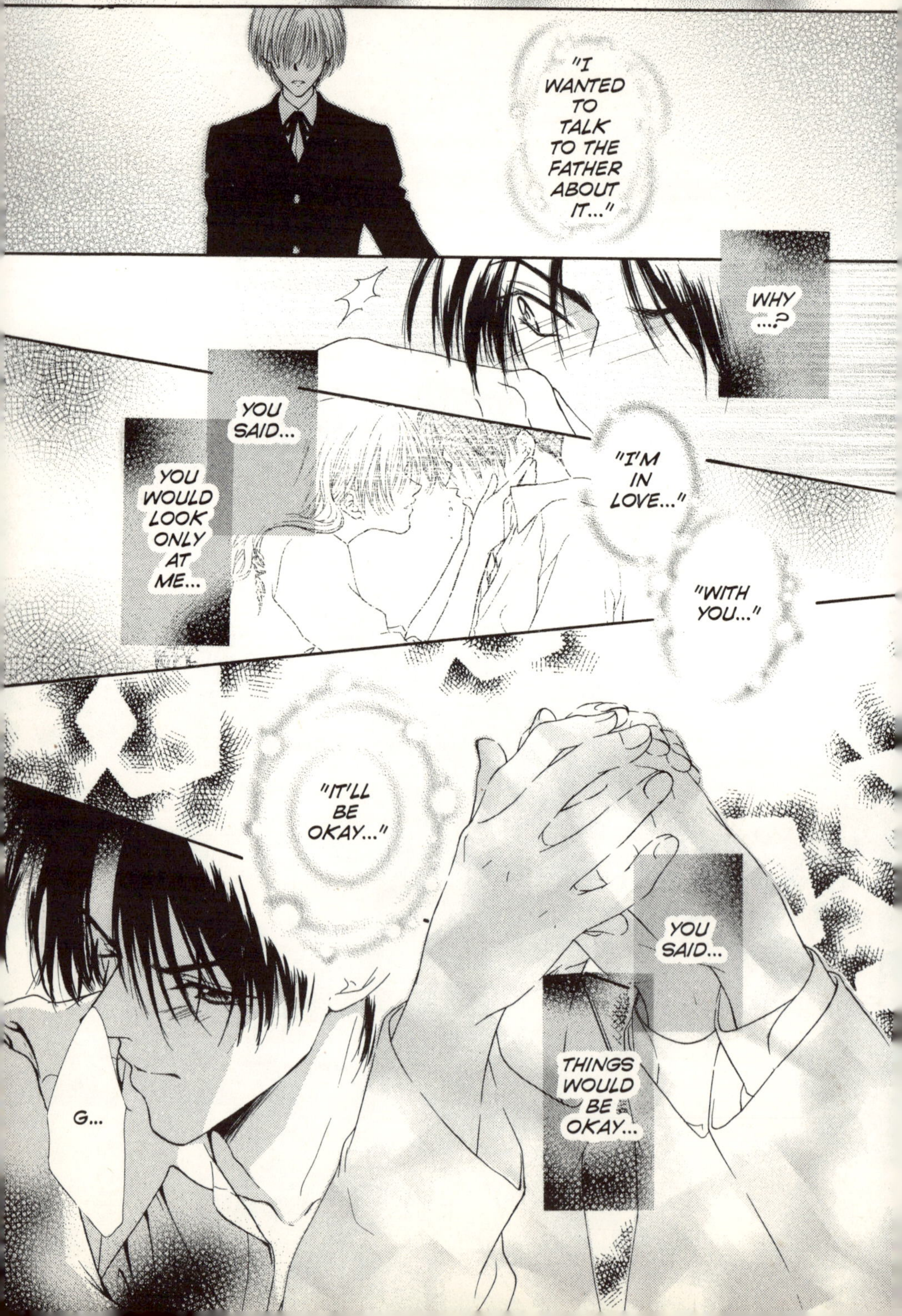
"I WANTED TO TALK TO THE FATHER ABOUT IT..."
WHY ...?
YOU SAID...
YOU WOULD LOOK ONLY AT ME...
"I'M IN LOVE..."
"WITH YOU..."
"IT'LL BE OKAY..."
YOU SAID...
THINGS WOULD BE OKAY...
G...

NOT AT GOD...
NOT AT LOUIS...
BUT AT ME...
ズキ...
PAN... ン...

IT'S A LIE...
WHY DON'T YOU SAVE HER ...!!
IT'S ALL A LIE !!

カッ…
TAP...
ン…
チャリ…
CHAK

"THAT'S FINE..."
カッ…
TAP...
BAM

HUFF...
......
HUFF...
CALM DOWN...
CREAK...
ギィィ...
IT'S NOT HER...
HUFF...

THUNK...
HUFF...
CLAK...
WH...
CLAK...
WHAT'S WRONG ...?
CLIK
CLAK
CLAK
CLAK...
WHERE'S LOUIS?
HUH?
I DON'T KNOW...
... ...
YOU...
YOU REALLY LIKE THIS GUY THAT MUCH?

WHAT ...?
LOVING HIM...
CLINGING TO HIM...
TRUSTING HIM...
DO YOU REALLY...
...LOVE HIM THAT MUCH ...?
SAVE HER--!!
I DON'T UNDER-STAND WHAT YOU'RE SAYING.
ISN'T THIS...
TAP...
TAP...
...JUST AN IMAGE ...?

TAP...
ROBERT?
WHY ...?
MY INTEREST IN HIM...
THIS EMPTY STATUE...
MY IRRITATION WITH HIM...
MY ANNOYANCE WITH HIM...
THIS THING THAT'S ONLY HERE FOR APPEARANCE...
THE REASON I CAN'T JUST LEAVE HIM ALONE...
IS IT REALLY WORTH PRAYING TO?
THIS THING...
IT'S JUST A FAKE...
IT'S ALL BECAUSE...
YOU'RE BEING FOOLED...
... ...
HE LOOKS LIKE HER...
THAT'S ALL...
THEN...

IF THIS FEEL-ING
IS A LIE...
THIS EMO-TION...
...IS AN ILLU-SION...
THEN...
IF ITS APPEAR-ANCE WERE TO CHANGE
...I WONDER... IF YOUR FEELINGS WOULD CHANGE, TOO...

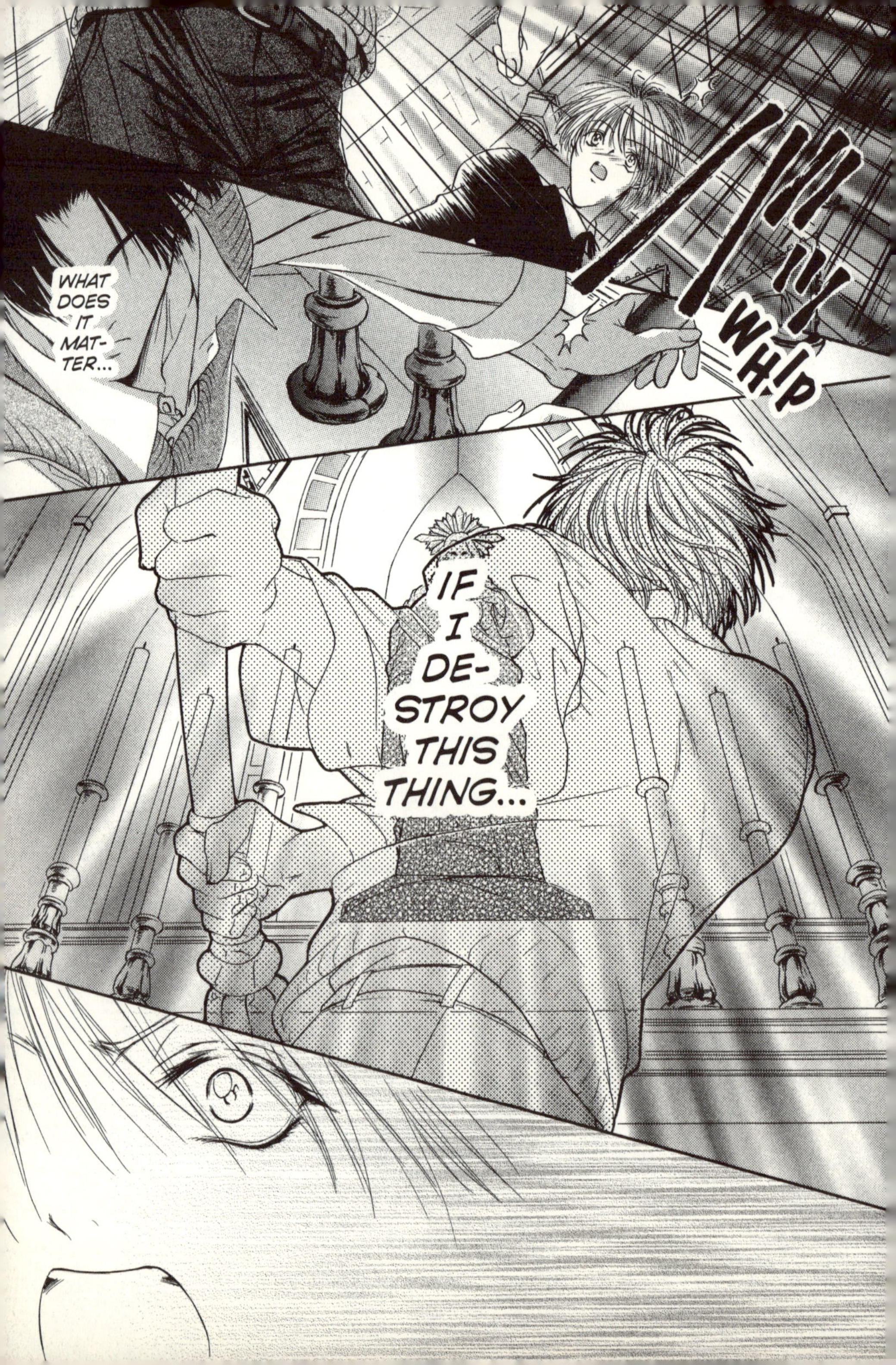
WHIP
WHAT DOES IT MAT-TER...
IF I DE-STROY THIS THING...

SMASH
RO-BERT?!
GROK
W...
WHAT ARE YOU...?!
!
WHAP
H...
IT'S JUST A STATUE, RIGHT?
"SHE WAS TOO BELOVED..."
THIS IS JUST AN IMITATION!
IT DOESN'T HAVE ANY REAL POWER AT ALL!
CRAK
"OF GOD..."
THWAK

STOP!
SHE HAD SO MUCH FAITH.
BAM
?!
CRASH
SMASH
WHEN PUSH COMES TO SHOVE, THIS GUY...
SHE HAD SO MUCH LOVE.
PLEASE!
STOP!
SHE WAS THE ONE...
RO-BERT!
FWOOSH
CRASH
...WON'T DO ANY-THING FOR YOU!
...WHO MOST DE-SERVED TO BE SAVED.
RO-BERT?!

PLEASE...
STOP...
WHY...
...I'M BEGGING YOU...
WHY CAN'T I WIN...?

WHAT IS IT...
......
...THAT MAKES YOU SO SAD?
WHAT ...?
SEE ...?
DON'T YOU LEAVE ME, TOO...
DON'T TAKE HIM AWAY...

I'M...
...RIGHT HERE.
PLEASE TELL ME...
YOU'RE...
...LEAVING ALREADY?
CLANG...

YES. IT WAS ONLY A TEMPORARY ASSIGNMENT, AFTER ALL.
HOW IS YOUR MOTHER?
WELL, FORTU-NATELY...
HER FEVER HAS GONE DOWN AND SHE'S DOING OKAY.
I SEE.
I'M GLAD.
WILL WE MEET AGAIN?
PERHAPS.
I MAY BE POSTED HERE ONE DAY...WHO KNOWS?
I'M AN ALUMNI OF THIS PLACE.
AND I'M ALSO CONCERNED ABOUT THE PUNISH-MENT...
...THAT WILL SOON BE HANDED DOWN TO HIM.
UM...

WHAT?
...IS THERE SOMETHING WRONG WITH MY FACE?
THE FIRST TIME WE MET...
...YOUR EXPRESSION CHANGED FOR AN INSTANT.
REALLY ...?
I'VE...
...BEEN TOLD SOMETHING SIMILAR BEFORE...
BY SOME-ONE ELSE...
"I CAN'T BELIEVE SOME-ONE LIKE YOU EXISTS..."
"THE THOUGHT OF THAT FACE OF YOURS WANDERING ALL OVER TOWN..."
BY ROBERT, TOO...

YOU KNOW EVERYTHING ABOUT HIM, DON'T YOU? FATHER LOUIS...?
......
IT MAY NOT BE FOR ME TO SAY...
IT'S JUST THAT HE...
HE'S LOST SOMEONE DEAR TO HIM IN THE PAST.
THAT PERSON, RESEMBLED YOU...
IN LOOKS, YES, BUT ALSO...
IN DEVOUTNESS... SOMETHING LIKE THAT.
YOU'RE VERY SIMILAR...
SO THAT...
...WAS...BECAUSE OF...ME...?

HA...
I'M ASHAMED.
I'M A BROTHER ONLY IN NAME...
I CAN'T BE OF ANY HELP TO HIM AT ALL.
I DON'T REALLY KNOW...
...WHAT WOULD BE BEST FOR HIM, BUT...
...PLEASE.

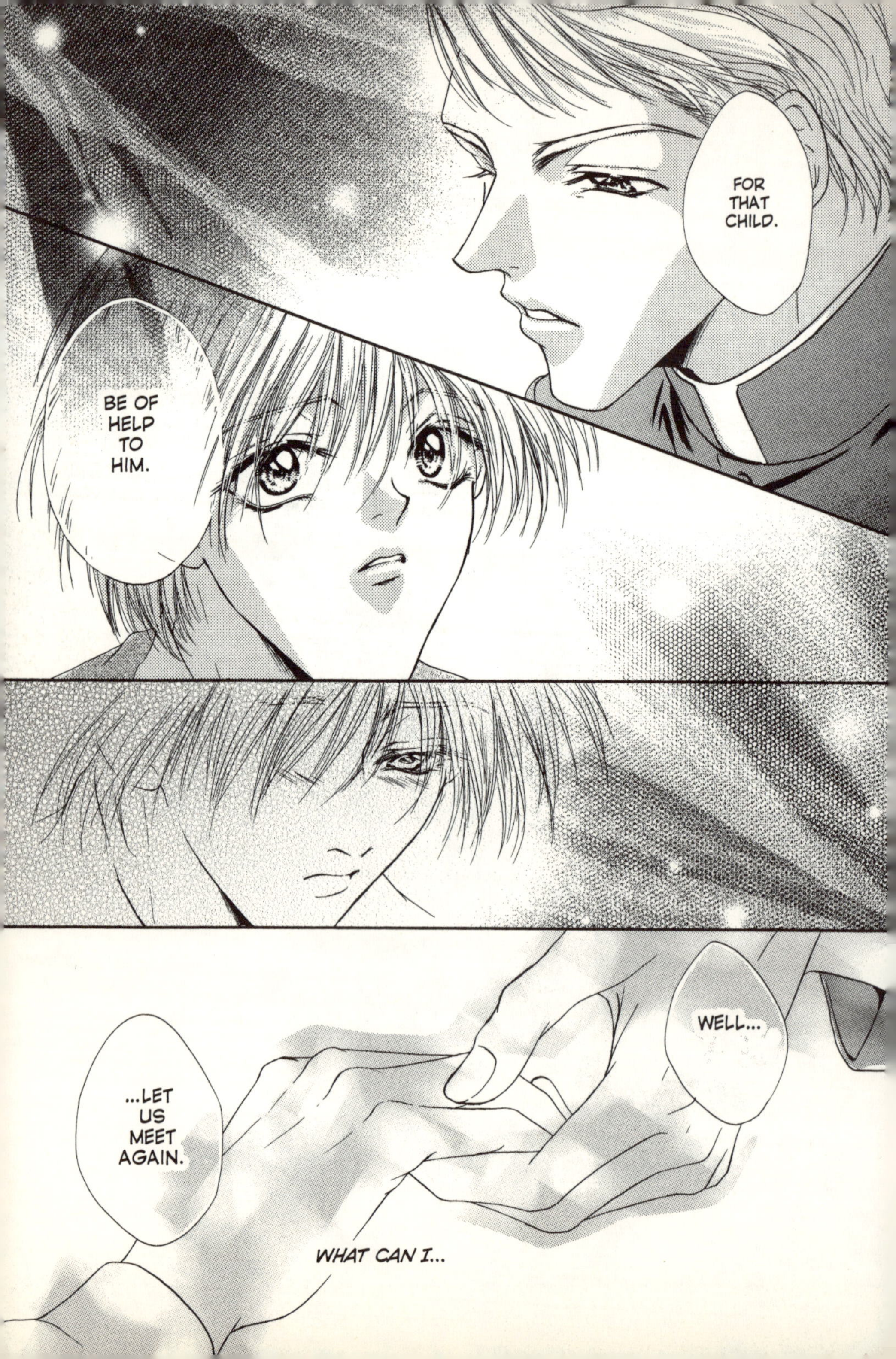
FOR THAT CHILD.
BE OF HELP TO HIM.
WELL...
...LET US MEET AGAIN.
WHAT CAN I...

TAKE CARE...
WHAT CAN I DO...?
RUSTLE...

WHOOSH

ARE YOU OKAY?
YOU FEEL FEVERISH.
I'M FINE.
I'M SORRY... I'LL FINISH UP AS SOON AS POSSIBLE.
HONK
UMM...
NOW, YOU MUSTN'T BE LIKE THAT.
YOU MUST BID YOUR MOTHER A PROPER GOOD-BYE.
BEEP
...NO...
YOUNG SIR...

NO!
ばっ
DASH
SIR!
!
ガッ
TA
A CERTAIN MEMORY...

キオク
MEMORY
OF A CERTAIN TIME...
OH!
OH NO!
IT'S ONE STATION FURTHER!
OH, BUT IT'S WITHIN WALKING DISTANCE.
パァー
HONK
RUN-NING...
HUH?

HE LOOKS FAST...
ぽ
STARE...
ピタ
THWAP
!
LET'S GO HOME.
WHY?
IT'S AN IMPORTANT ERRAND, RIGHT?
I CAN COME BACK.
NO, I'M OKAY.
...BE-CAUSE OF ME.
ふるふる
SHAKE SHAKE
I DON'T WANT MOTHER TO WORRY...
IT'S TROUBLESOME TO COME ALL THE WAY OUT HERE AGAIN, ISN'T IT?
I'M FINE.
SO...
...OKAY.

BUT MAKE SURE TO TELL ME IF YOU START TO FEEL UNWELL.
ざわ MURMUR
OKAY.
ざわ MURMUR
ざわ MURMUR
カラン… TINKLE…
WELCOME.
OH, YES--HE DOES LIVE UPSTAIRS HERE.
BUT HE'S OUT...HE WON'T RETURN UNTIL TOMORROW.
I SEE...
I'M SORRY YOU TOOK ALL THE TROUBLE...
NO, I SHOULD HAVE CALLED FIRST.
THEN SHALL I GIVE HIM A MESSAGE?
YES.

OH...
YES, THAT'S RIGHT.
THEN COULD YOU JUST TELL HIM THAT?
YES, I UNDERSTAND.
YOU VERY MUCH.
WE'RE GOING NOW.
WHAT'S WRONG?
NOTH-ING...
MURMUR
MURMUR
MURMUR

BUMP
MURMUR
THAT'S THE BIG CITY FOR YOU...
MURMUR
MURMUR
ARE YOU ALL RIGHT, GEORGES?
GEORGES?
DAZED
HUH?
LET'S SIT DOWN FOR A BIT.
THERE'S A BENCH OVER THERE.
HA HA HA HA
BE CARE-FUL!

ALL RIGHT?
I'M GOING TO GO GET SOME JUICE OVER THERE...
SO YOU SIT HERE AND WAIT FOR ME, OKAY?
OKAY...
DON'T LEAVE THIS SPOT, OKAY?
...OK...
ほけ。
DAZED
た…
TA...
きゃはは…
HA HA HA...
CARRY ME!
ALL RIGHT, ALL RIGHT.

CARRY ME!
CARRY ME!
OOH, YOU'RE HEAVY.
GRANDMA'S GOING TO FALL OVER!
きゃっ GIGGLE
きゃっ SQUEAL
きゃは HA HA は HA は HA
HERE YA GO!
SORRY FOR THE WAIT!
THANK YOU.
WHAT'LL IT BE?
THIS, PLEASE.
GEORGES?

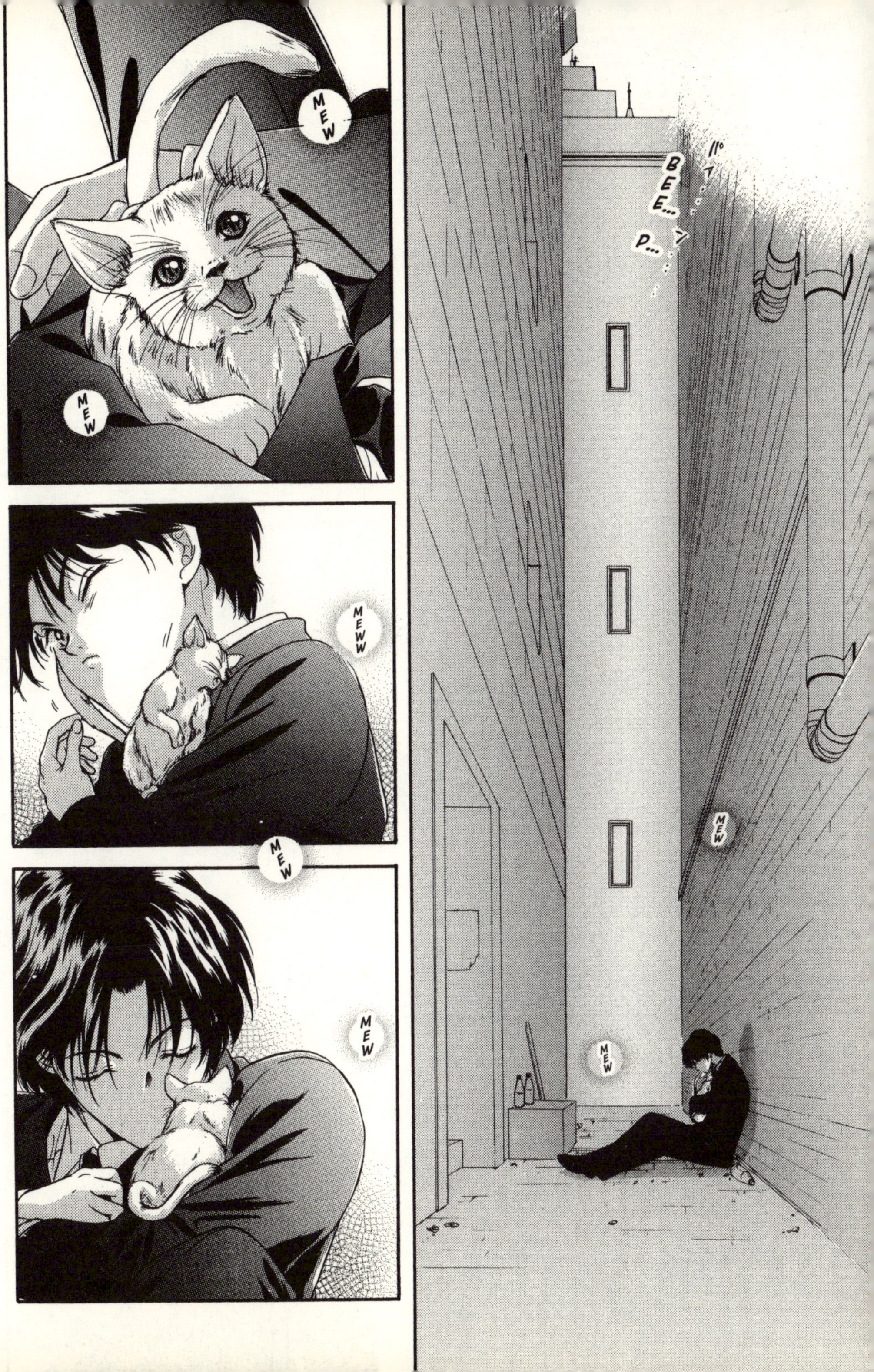
BEE...
P...
MEW
MEW
MEW
MEW
MEWW
MEW
MEW

MEOW
ビクン
FLINCH!
OH!
JUMP
ニャアー
MEOWW
MEOW
TA TA TA TA
MEW

PURR
PURR
PURR
DASH
CLANK
HMPH...
"TODAY IS YOUR MOTHER'S FUNERAL..."
"THAT'S NOT MY MOTHER!"
HUFF...

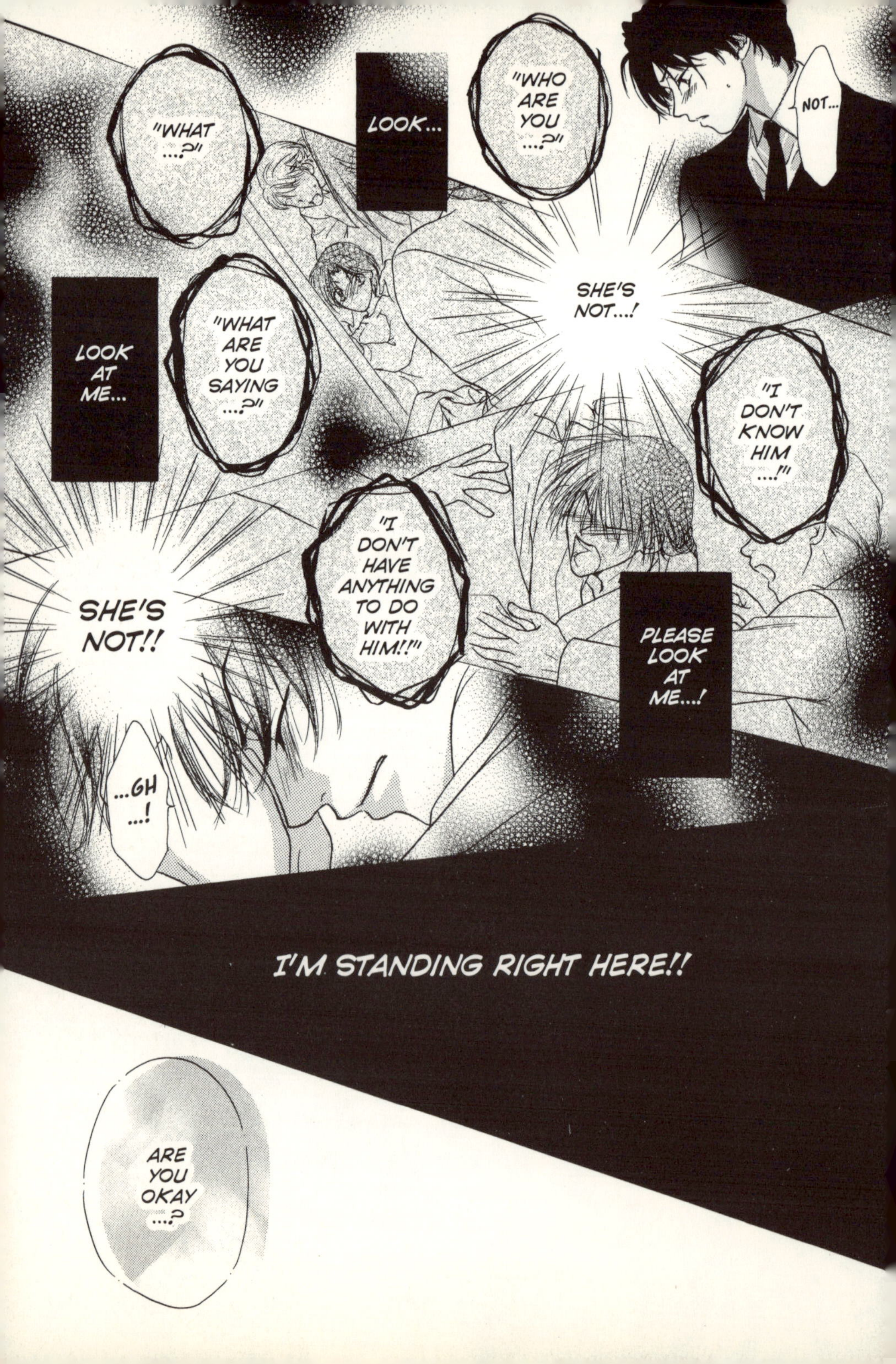

NOT...
"WHO ARE YOU ...?"
LOOK...
"WHAT ...?"
SHE'S NOT...!
LOOK AT ME...
"WHAT ARE YOU SAYING ...?"
"I DON'T KNOW HIM ...!"
"I DON'T HAVE ANYTHING TO DO WITH HIM!!"
PLEASE LOOK AT ME...!
SHE'S NOT!!
...GH ...!
I'M STANDING RIGHT HERE!!
ARE YOU OKAY ...?

WHOOSH
DO YOU FEEL BAD ...?

WHAT ...?
UMM...
THIS KID...
WHAT...
WHAT... DO YOU WANT...
CLINK...
WHO ARE YOU...
UM...
YOUR GRANDMOTHER
FWIP
JUMP!
I THINK SHE'S LOOKING FOR YOU.
IS HE TALKING ABOUT HANNA ...?
GRANDMOTHER ...?
WHA?
UMM...
YOU SEE...
I THINK YOU RUN *REALLY* FAST.

THAT'S WHY...
YOUR GRAND-MOTHER...
...SHE CAN'T CATCH UP TO YOU.
IS THAT ALL ...?
... ...
UM, SO I THINK YOU SHOULD GO BACK.
YOU DON'T LIKE...
...YOUR GRAND-MOTHER?
NO.
DON'T STARE UP AT ME!
WHY?
FLINCH!
BECAUSE I DON'T WANT TO!
PEEK

THAT'S NOT IT!
I'M NOT TALKING ABOUT HANNA!
MY MOTHE--
JOLT
SOMEONE LIKE THAT...
SHE ISN'T MY...
HUH?
THAT'S NOT... A PARENT...
SHE DOESN'T...
EVEN SEE ME...
SHE DOESN'T EVEN...
...RECOGNIZE ME.
I TELL YOU, I DON'T KNOW HIM!!
SMASH

"GET OUT!!"
GH...
SHE'S NOT...
...NOT...

IT'S OKAY...
WHAT...
EVERY-THING WILL BE OKAY...
YOU SEE,
GOD IS ALWAYS WATCHING OVER US ALL.
WHAT'S...
THIS ...?
BA-THUM

THAT'S WHY
I'M SURE...
...HE'S WATCHING OVER YOU, TOO.
BA-THUMP...
I'VE NEVER KNOWN...
BA-THUMP...
HE IS.
HE'S SURE TO FIND YOU...
...SOME-THING LIKE THIS...
BA-THUMP...
CLAK...
SO LET'S GO.
TOGETHER.
HUFF...
BA-THUMP...
BA-THUMP...
I'M SCARED...

WHACK

は…
HAH!
OW...
JOLT!
BA-THUM
H...
HIC
WAAH...

THANK YOU...
!
ぱっ
DASH
HUFF...
HUFF...
HUFF...

SIR!!
OH...
I'M SO GLAD!!
T T T
WHEW!
YOU'VE SHORTENED POOR HANNA'S LIFE!
IF SOMETHING WERE TO HAPPEN TO YOU ON AN IMPORTANT DAY LIKE TODAY...!
HUFF...
SIR?
IT'S BE-CAUSE ...!

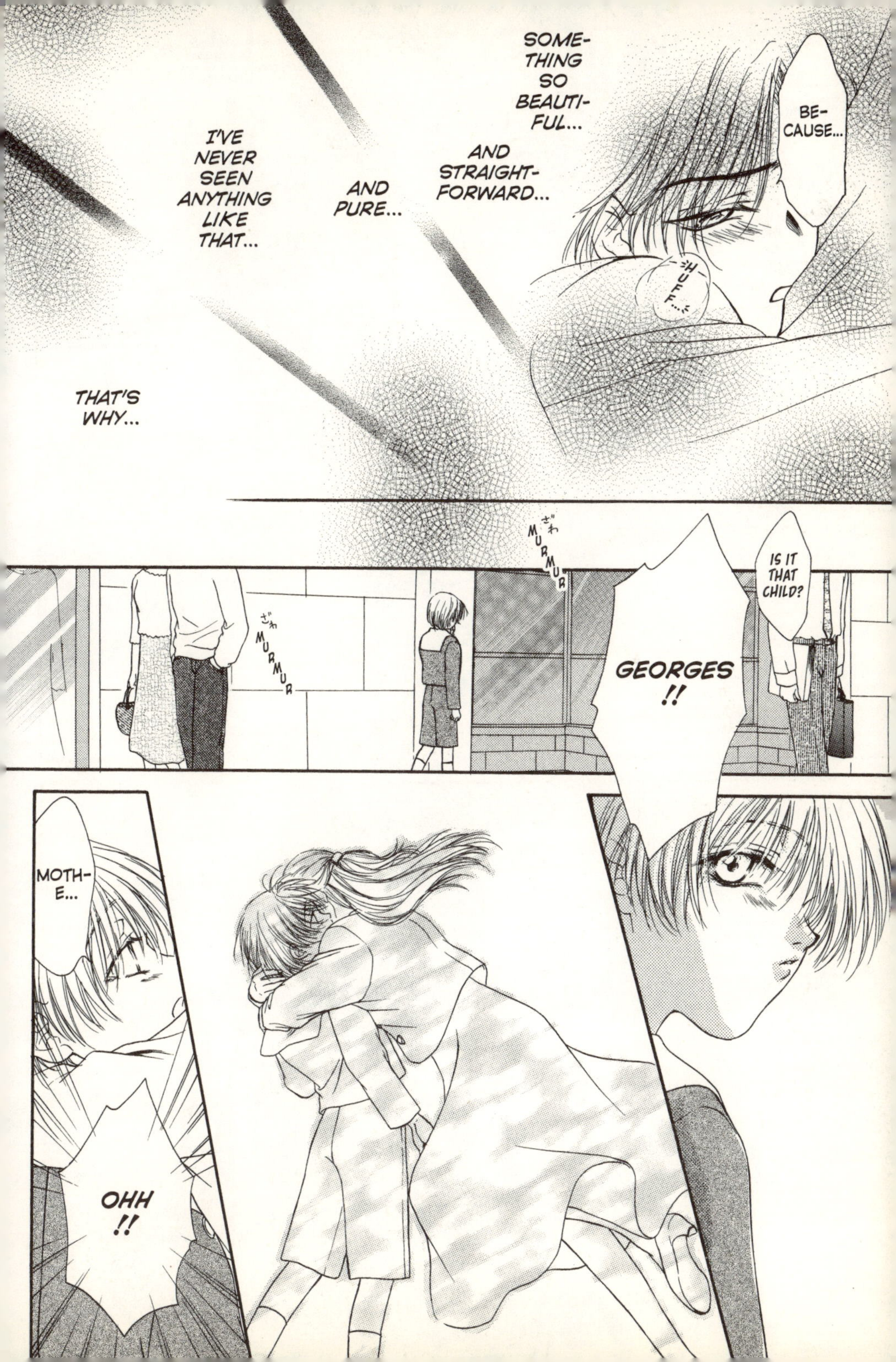
BE-
CAUSE...
HUFF...
SOME-
THING
SO
BEAUTI-
FUL...
AND
STRAIGHT-
FORWARD...
AND
PURE...
I'VE
NEVER
SEEN
ANYTHING
LIKE
THAT...
THAT'S
WHY...
IS IT
THAT
CHILD?
MURMUR
GEORGES
!!
MURMUR
MOTH-
E...
OHH
!!

WHERE HAVE YOU BEEN ?!
I TOLD YOU STAY PUT!
OH NO...
YOU'RE BURNING UP...
AHH ...!
WHAT HAPPENED ?!
THIS ...!
THIS WOUND ...!
OHH...
HOW COULD THIS HAPPEN...
ぎゅ..
SQUEEZE...
MOTH... ER ...?
HOW COULD I...
OH...
SHE'S GOING TO CRY...
--RY...

I'M SORRY...
ふぇ~... WAAH...
HIC...
HIC.
IT'S OKAY...
EVERY-THING'S OKAY...
KLUP
KLUP
KLUP
KLUP
...AND THEN,
YOU JUST COLLAPSED.

WHEN YOU WOKE UP, I ASKED YOU WHAT HAPPENED AND YOU SAID YOU COULDN'T REMEMBER...
SO I NEVER DID FIND OUT.
THANK GOODNESS IT WASN'T A SERIOUS WOUND...
BUT I WAS REALLY WORRIED ABOUT YOU!
REALLY ...?
I SURE HAVE A BAD MEMORY.
I DON'T REMEMBER THAT AT ALL...
IT'S BECAUSE YOU WERE HAZY FROM THE FEVER.
NONE OF IT WOULD HAVE HAPPENED IF WE'D JUST COME STRAIGHT HOME.
IT'S OKAY... I DON'T REMEMBER ANYTHING ANYWAY.
AND IT WAS MY FAULT...
OH!
LOOK AT THE TIME!
DON'T YOU HAVE TO GO?
CLATTER
OH NO!
YOU'RE RIGHT! I'LL BE LATE!
OKA-A-AY!
BE CARE-FUL!
TA...

A CERTAIN MEMORY...
ん HMM...
OF A CERTAIN TIME...
ガチャ KCHAK...
OH WELL.
I'M OFF.
YOUNG SIR!
HURRY!
YOU'RE GOING TO BE LATE!

STOP CALLING ME THAT ALREADY.
THAT "YOUNG SIR"...
OH?
HOW ELSE SHOULD I ADDRESS YOU?
YOUNG SIR IS YOUNG SIR.
PLEASE DON'T DAWDLE JUST BECAUSE YOU KNOW THE MASTER'S NOT HERE!
HANNA IS THE ONE WHO IS GOING TO BE SCOLDED!
OK, OK.
I'M ALWAYS LIKE THIS, THOUGH.
THE ELDERLY SURE ARE FUSSY.
YOUNG SIR!!
OOH!
EEP!
SURELY...
CLANG...

CLANG...
ROBERT!
MORNING!
YO.
...A MEMORY THAT WILL SOON REAWAKE.
Memory ◆ END

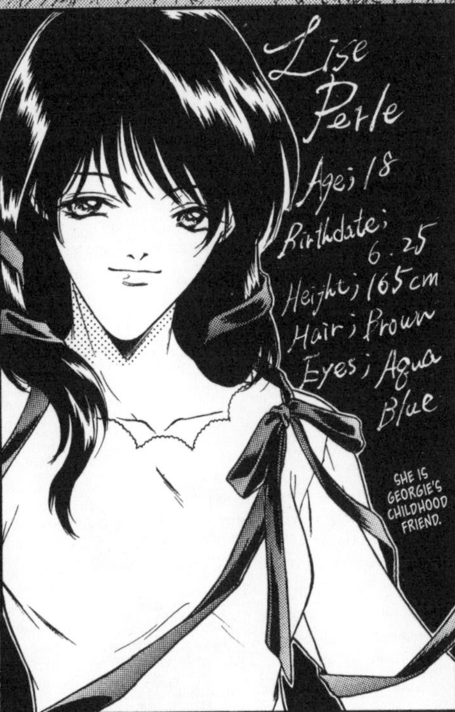

PROMENADE THREE

HELLO. THIS IS CHIGUSA KAWAI. AND THIS IS VOLUME 3 OF "LA ESPERANCA".

IT HAS BEEN A WHOLE YEAR SINCE THE RELEASE OF VOLUME 2--FOR THOSE OF YOU WHO WAITED, I APOLOGIZE. BUT AFTER VOLUME 2'S RELEASE I WAS TOLD, "IT CAME OUT FASTER THAN I EXPECTED," SO PERHAPS A YEAR'S WAIT IS NOT SO UNUSUAL AFTER ALL...? NO, A YEAR SEEMS PRETTY LONG...HMM...AFTER ALL THIS TIME, I STILL DON'T KNOW MUCH ABOUT THIS INDUSTRY... ANYWAY, THANK YOU FOR TAKING THIS BOOK IN HAND. I KNOW THAT SOME OF YOU START BY READING THE AFTERWORD FIRST SO I WON'T SAY TOO MUCH, BUT VARIOUS LOOSE ENDS ARE TIED UP IN THIS VOLUME 3. I HOPE YOU ENJOY IT. (I'M THE TYPE WHO STARTS BY READING THE AFTERWORD, BY THE WAY.)

@ CHAPTER 7 - THE SUMMONING BELL PT.1 AND PT.2 (LISE'S TALE)

→ AS I WAS TRYING TO DEVELOP ARTHUR'S CHARACTER, I THOUGHT OF THIS GUY WHO DRIVES OUT TO OUR HOUSE EVERY WEEK TO SELL BREAD--AND SO I DECIDED, "LET'S MAKE HIM A BAKER!" THE BREAD GUY AND ARTHUR ARE TOTALLY DIFFERENT PERSONALITIES, AND THE REAL PERSON IS, TO THIS DAY, A CURIOUSLY ANONYMOUS CHARACTER OF INDETERMINATE AGE.

@ CHAPTER 8 - ICON PT.1 AND PT. 2 (BROTHER LOUIS' TALE)

→ I REALLY WORKED HARD ON THOSE WHITE ROSES IN THE COLOR SECTION!! BUT YOU CAN'T EVEN TELL IN BLACK AND WHITE!! ONCE, WHEN I WAS WORKING ON THE ART AT NIGHT, I REMEMBER SUDDENLY BEING OVERCOME WITH SADNESS AND CRYING...NOW I CAN'T EVEN REMEMBER WHAT I WAS SAD ABOUT...MAYBE I WAS JUST SLEEPY... (WHAT AM I, A LITTLE KID?!)

@ EXTRA EPISODE (?) - MEMORY (THE CHIBI CHARACTERS' TALE)

→ THIS WAS MY FIRST 32-PAGE STANDALONE EPISODE IN A WHILE AND IT WAS REFRESHING. I'M NOT REALLY SURE IF I CAN CALL THIS AN EXTRA EPISODE...THERE WERE QUITE A FEW PEOPLE CHARMED TO DEATH BY THE CHIBI-GEORGIE CHARACTER. "IF HE REALLY EXISTED, I WOULD'VE KIDNAPPED HIM BY NOW!!!" (SAID A FRIEND OF MINE) WHY YOU...!

THE SEASON AT THIS POINT IN THE STORY IS JUST BEFORE SUMMER VACATION. AT THE END OF THAT VACATION (THERE'S AN ADVANCEMENT EXAM BEFORE THAT, BUT...), GEORGES AND THE OTHERS WILL BE IN THEIR SECOND YEAR OF HIGH SCHOOL. YES, THAT'S RIGHT--THEY'RE HIGH SCHOOL FRESHMEN. IN THIS STORY WORLD, HIGH SCHOOL LASTS FOR FOUR YEARS. SO IT'S NOT 6-3-3 BUT 5-3-4. TO EVERYONE WHO THOUGHT THE CHARACTERS WERE IN JUNIOR HIGH, I'M SORRY. TECHNICALLY, ACCORDING TO AGE, THEY WOULD BE IN JUNIOR HIGH. INCIDENTALLY, THE JUNIOR HIGH UNIFORMS ARE THE ONES ERWIN AND JOSHUA ARE WEARING IN VOLUME 2. (CHIBI-GEORGIE IS WEARING THE ELEMENTARY SCHOOL DIVISION UNIFORM IN THAT SAME VOLUME.) "WHY 4 YEARS?!" YOU ASK? WELL, BECAUSE IF GEORGES WAS IN HIS THIRD YEAR OF JUNIOR HIGH, GRADUATION WOULD BE JUST AROUND THE CORNER--A LOT OF CHANGES WOULD HAVE TO BE MADE AND IT JUST SEEMED LIKE IT WOULD BE A LOT OF WORK! THAT WAS THE MAIN REASON...AND I WANTED HIM TO BE 14 YEARS OLD... I DON'T KNOW WHY...

TO ALL OF YOU WHO TELL ME, "I READ THE MAGAZINE, TOO," HERE IS AN ANNOUNCEMENT: THE NEXT STORY AFTER THE ONES PUBLISHED IN THIS VOLUME 3 WILL NOW BE SERIALIZED IN "WINGS" MAGAZINE. I HOPE YOUR SUPPORT WILL CONTINUE AS ALWAYS.

TO EVERYONE WHO SENDS ME LETTERS, THANK YOU. THEY ARE MY "SOURCE OF ENERGY". ALL THE ILLUSTRATIONS AND PRESENTS YOU'VE SENT ME ARE PROMINENTLY DISPLAYED IN AREAS WHERE I CAN VIEW THEM WHILE WORKING. OCCASIONALLY I'LL BE SENT PAPERS AND THINGS THAT ARE PRINTED ON A WHIM, AND FOR THOSE, PLEASE BE SURE TO INCLUDE A RETURN ADDRESS. (PLEASE, BY ALL MEANS! THERE ARE STILL OCCASIONALLY SOME WHO DON'T INCLUDE IT!)

WELL, I GUESS THAT'S IT FOR VOLUME 3. THANK YOU VERY MUCH FOR READING ♥ LET'S MEET AGAIN! '02 APR CHERRY BLOSSOMS IN FULL BLOOM!

Chigusa Kawai

Special Thanks to
"K"TANI-SAMA, OCHI-SAMA...AND YOU.

TIME LAG
A LOVE LETTER...
Delivered THREE
years later...
Can love bring Satoru and Shirou
together, even after all this time?
ISBN#1-56970-921-1 $12.95
Time Lag © 1999, 2000 by Shinobu GOTOH and Hotaru ODAGIRI.
All rights reserved. Original Japanese edition
published by TOKUMA SHOTEN PUBLISHING CO., LTD.
June™
junemanga.com

微熱革命
YUKINE HONAMI
SERUBO SUZUKI
SWEET REVOLUTION
WHAT CAN BE SWEETER THAN
FORBIDDEN LOVE?
ISBN# 1-56970-910-6 $12.95
© 2000 Yukine Honami / Serubo Suzuki. All rights reserved.
First published in Japan in 2000 by HOUBUNSHA CO.LTD., Tokyo.
English translation rights in United States and Canada arranged with
HOUBUNSHA CO., LTD. through Tuttle-Mori Agency, Inc. Tokyo.
June™
junemanga.com

SAME CELL ORGANISM
by Sumomo Yumeka
Different... yet alike...
How can two people be so completely different from one another, yet be so in tune with love?
June™ by DMP
junemanga.com
ISBN: 1-56970-926-2 $12.95
Same-Cell Organism/Dousaibou Seibutsu © Sumomo Yumeka 2001.
Originally published in Japan in 2001 by Taiyo Tosho Co., Ltd.

OUR KINGDOM
When the Prince falls for the Pauper...
The family inheritance will be the last of their concerns.
Written & Illustrated by
Naduki Koujima
Volume 1 ISBN# 1-56970-935-1 $12.95
Volume 2 ISBN# 1-56970-914-9 $12.95
Volume 3 ISBN# 1-56970-913-0 $12.95
Volume 4 ISBN# 1-56970-912-2 $12.95
DMP
DIGITAL MANGA PUBLISHING
yaoi-manga.com
The girls only sanctuary
Our Kingdom © 2000 Naduki Koujima

Hybrid Child
by Shungiki Nakamura
Half machine...
Half human...
What can your Hybrid Child do for you?
June™
junemanga.com
ISBN# 1-56970-902-5 $12.95
Hybrid Child © Shungiku Nakamura 2005.
Originally published in Japan in 2005 by BIBLOS Co. Ltd.

Written and Illustrated by
You Higuri
A desperate search…
In the garden of the sacred beast…
Gorgeous Carat Galaxy
Danger awaits those who dare to enter.
ISBN# 1-56970-903-3 $12.95
Gorgeous Carat Galaxy © You Higur 2004. Originally published in Japan in 2004 by GENTOSHA Comics Inc., Tokyo.
June™
junemanga.com

THE DAY OF REVOLUTION

MIKIYO TSUDA

DMP
IGITAL MANGA
PUBLISHING

ISBN# 1-56970-889-4 $12.95

WHO AM I?
COLD SLEEP
a novel
by Narise Konohara
Having lost his memory in an accident, Toru Takahisa tries to reclaim his past. Fujishima is the man that takes Toru in, claiming to be his friend. Find out what happens in this exciting new novel.
DMP
DIGITAL MANGA PUBLISHING
yaoi-manga.com
The girls only sanctuary
ISBN# 1-56970-887-8 $8.95
© Narise Konohara 2003. Originally published in Japan in 2003 by BIBLOS Co., Ltd.

STO

This is the back of the book!
Start from the other side.

NATIVE MANGA readers read manga from *right to left*.

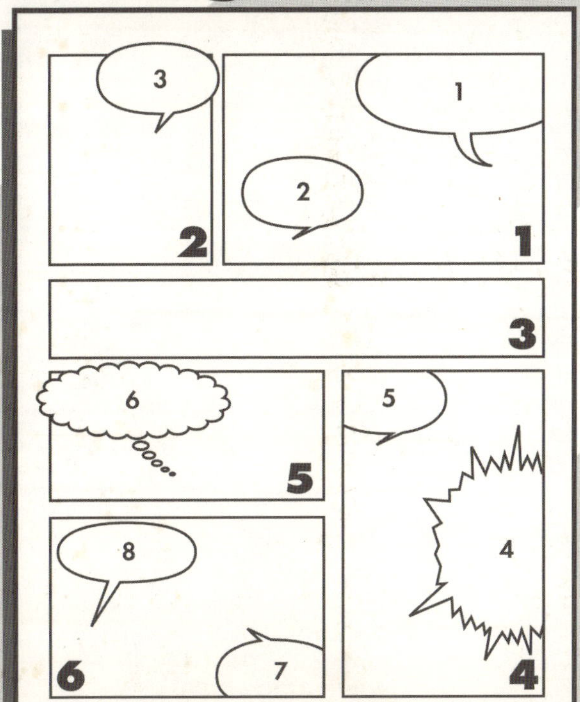

If you run into our ***Native Manga*** *logo on any of our books... you'll know that this manga is published in it's true original native Japanese right to left reading format, as it was intended. Turn to the other side of the book and start reading from right to left, top to bottom.*

Follow the diagram to see how its done.
Surf's Up!

NATIVE MANGA
READ RIGHT TO LEFT